RUNEMAKER

⌘

Other books by Tiina Nunnally

Fiction

Maija, a novel

Selected Translations

Niels Lyhne by Jens Peter Jacobsen
Mogens & Other Stories by Jens Peter Jacobsen
Night Roamers & Other Stories by Knut Hamsun
Katinka by Herman Bang
Laterna Magica by William Heinesen
The Faces by Tove Ditlevsen
Early Spring by Tove Ditlevsen

Tiina Nunnally

Runemaker

⌘

A Margit Andersson Mystery

Fjord Press
Seattle

This is a work of fiction. Names, characters, places, and occurrences are either the product of the author's imagination or are used fictitiously. Any resemblance to actual persons, events, or locales is purely coincidental.

Published and distributed by:
Fjord Press, PO Box 16349, Seattle, WA 98116
tel (206) 935-7376 / fax (206) 938-1991 / email: fjord@halcyon.com

Editor: Steven T. Murray
Design & typography: Fjord Press
Cover design: Jane Fleming
Cover illustrations: Motifs from the Golden Horns sketched by
    J.R. Paulli, 1734
Photograph of the Golden Horns used by permission of
    Nationalmuseet, Copenhagen, Denmark
Author photograph: Mike Bennett

Excerpt from "The Golden Horns" by Adam Oehlenschlæger (1802), translated from the Danish by Robert Silliman Hillyer (New York: American-Scandinavian Foundation, 1922)

Printed on recycled alkaline paper by Thomson & Shore, Dexter, Michigan

Library of Congress Cataloging in Publication Data:
Nunnally, Tiina, 1952–
    Runemaker : a Margit Andersson mystery / Tiina Nunnally. —
1st ed.
        p.   cm.
    ISBN 0-940242-77-X (trade paperback)
    I. Title.
PS3564.U53R86   1996
813´.54—dc20   96-28795
                                                    CIP

Printed in the United States of America
First edition, 1996

For Steve,
who wanted me to write a mystery

RUNEMAKER

⌘

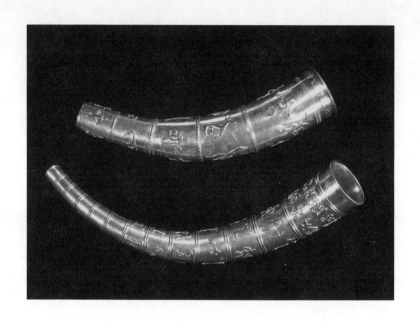

The hour strikes; the gods have given;
Now the gods have taken back;
Storms crash; the clouds are riven;
The relics vanish in the black.

— Adam Oehlenschlæger

1

I t was the first day of spring, and at 7:30 in the morning the
sky was still a flat gray, with no sign of the sunbreaks promised by the local weather forecasters. Margit Andersson sighed
heavily, wishing she was back in New Mexico with Joe, driving
north through O'Keeffe country instead of vying for space in the
narrow lanes of Seattle's Aurora Bridge. She glanced in the rearview mirror and frowned at the weary look in her blue eyes. It
was always hard to get back into the swing of the regular work
week after a vacation, and the gloomy weather wasn't making
the transition any easier. Margit switched on her headlights,
turned up the volume on the tape deck, and tucked a loose
strand of blonde hair behind her ear. She was not a person given
to premonitions, or she might have had some warning that this
day was about to start off so horribly.

⌘

Margit had gotten in late from Santa Fe the night before. It was
almost ten p.m. by the time she claimed her car from the airport

parking lot and drove home to her small house in West Seattle. Her huge black cat, Gregor, emerged from the bushes as she pulled into the driveway. He rubbed up against the rear tires and sniffed the undercarriage of the twelve-year-old dented silver Mazda to see where his vehicle had been all week. Margit bent down to pick him up, nuzzling his resistant bulk, and finally set him back down on the pavement with a laugh. Gregor was not a cuddly cat, but he was good company nonetheless, and she could tell that he had missed her. He raced past her up the walkway, always determined to be the first through the door. And no doubt he was looking for some kind of treat, knowing that she would pamper him after being gone a whole week.

Margit unlocked the door and dropped her suitcase and shoulder bag next to the sofa. Her friend Renny Latham had been looking after the house, and she had left the floor lamp in the corner turned on, as well as the overhead light in the dining room. There was a note propped against a bottle of white wine on the oak table.

"Welcome back. Everything fine," it said. "Gregor was his usual rowdy self. He ate the begonia in the bedroom and broke the blue bowl that was on the coffee table. I got the grant— thanks to you! Here's a bottle of wine to celebrate. See you later in the week."

Margit smiled. She had ended up writing that whole grant proposal for Renny, who was a brilliant painter but had trouble putting her ideas into words. Two days before the deadline for the Puget Foundation arts awards, Renny had called Margit in despair, complaining that she had been trying to write the proposal for three weeks and just couldn't do it. Renny was convinced that Sandra Dalkovitch was going to get the grant again—and she was a terrible painter, a real amateur, doing nothing but sentimental and derivative work. But Sandra was a tireless self-promoter, and her name was always in the paper.

"I'm sick and tired of losing out on all the big awards," Renny told Margit. This time she was determined to snag one for herself. She would show those critics, who kept labeling her an "emerging artist" even though she'd been painting for over twenty years. Renny was convinced that she was stuck with this beginner's label because she was black. Even the most mediocre white painters were described as being in "mid-career" by the time they were Renny's age. And she already had several highly successful shows to her name.

"You're a writer, Margit," Renny had said on the phone. "Couldn't you help me with this grant proposal? Please? I'm really desperate."

"OK, bring it over and I'll have a look at it, but I'll tell you right now that I don't know much about painting," Margit had said. She was flattered to hear Renny call her a writer. So few people recognized that the translation work she did for a living required just as much writing skill as it did linguistic ability.

Apparently Margit's efforts had done the job.

Good, she thought, Renny deserves the money. Now she can cut back on her hours at the café and spend more time on her painting.

Margit went into the kitchen and switched on the light over the sink, taking a can of Kitty Stew out of the cupboard next to the fridge. She didn't usually feed beef to her cat. Margit was a vegetarian herself, although occasionally she did eat fish. She could accept the fact that cats were carnivores, but she couldn't quite picture Gregor bringing down a steer with one mighty leap at its throat, ready to administer his fiercest bite of death. She thought it was more natural for him to eat fish and chicken, prey of a more manageable size. But Renny had once offered Kitty Stew to Gregor, and he had whined at the tuna on his plate for days afterwards. Beef had clearly become his dinner of choice. On special occasions, Margit would relent and get out the stew.

She plopped a heaping portion of the malodorous mud onto a red plastic plate and set it on the floor next to the stove. Gregor growled happily and started lapping up the food. He had a peculiar habit of talking while he ate, grunting and purring contentedly.

"Don't talk with your mouth full," Margit said affectionately as she left the room. "And sit down and relax. Don't eat like a dog."

She snapped on the desk lamp in her study and punched the play button on the answering machine. Only three messages in a whole week. Guess she hadn't missed much.

"Margit, where the hell are you? It's Tuesday, and we've got a rush job from Thor Cheese, and the VP is breathing down my neck. Needs it ASAP before he gets on the plane tomorrow for Copenhagen. I can't get hold of Lars either. By the way, there are a couple of things in that salmon job I want to discuss with you. Do you really think that 'preliminary' is the right word? Call me back."

Margit grimaced. She distinctly remembered telling her boss Liisa that she would be out of town for a week. Determining her own schedule was the only benefit she had as a freelancer working for the Koivisto Translation Agency. No sick leave, no paid vacations, and she had to pay for her own health insurance too. Sometimes she wondered why she had ever given up her secure job with an international import company for the freelance life.

Here she was, forty years old and still scrambling to pay the mortgage each month. But she had her freedom, and she wasn't stuck behind a desk eight hours a day, with the boss's secretary on the alert to make sure she didn't take a few extra minutes for lunch. Margit treasured her independence, and she liked working alone at home, only going into the agency for meetings and occasional jobs that required her to be there. Margit worked for several other clients, including a company in L.A., but for the past two years the Koivisto Translation Agency had been her bread and butter. So she tended to think of Liisa as her boss—an impression that Liisa unequivocally encouraged.

When Margit needed a breather from the technical translation work that consumed so much of her time, she would tell Liisa to take her off the available list for a few days. But when she wasn't working, she wasn't bringing in any money either, so her vacations were always rare events.

Liisa must have forgotten that Margit would be in New Mexico for the week. She sounded frantic, as usual. Probably had to translate the cheese job herself if she couldn't get Lars to do it. And of course she *would* find something wrong with that salmon article Margit had done.

All the freelancers dreaded Liisa's request for a "discussion" of their work, but it was Margit and Lars who suffered the real brunt of her perfection mania, since Liisa was a Swedish Finn and could read the Scandinavian languages herself. She never failed to go over their translations, checking them line by line against the original, even after an editor and a proofreader had already approved their work. All the extra time she spent on their jobs must have cut into the agency's profits. Margit had once surreptitiously taped a Far Side cartoon to her boss's door—the one where Einstein discovers that time is actually money—but Liisa didn't get the joke. The freelancers all decided that having to deal with scores of demanding clients over the past ten years had stunted their boss's sense of humor.

The second caller on Margit's answering machine had hung up without leaving a message—something that always annoyed her.

And the third message was from Søren Rasmussen, an eighty-year-old fisherman Margit had befriended a couple of months back, when the agency got a call for a Danish interpreter at Harborview Hospital and she had agreed to take on the assignment.

Even though the Koivisto Translation Agency made a large share of its income by providing interpreters to the local hospitals and courts, it was rare to get a request for one of the Nordic languages. The biggest demand was for Vietnamese, Laotian, Korean, Mandarin, and lately Russian, reflecting the recent wave of immigrants to the Pacific Northwest. Most Scandinavians who lived in the area had arrived at least thirty or forty years ago, and their English was perfectly understandable, although some had a stronger accent than others. When they spoke their native language, however, it could sometimes be nearly unintelligible, a crazy mishmash of archaic colloquialisms and American words with Scandinavian endings—what Margit and Lars liked to call Danglish, Swenglish, and Norglish.

When Margit showed up at the emergency room of Harborview Hospital, the nurse at the admitting desk ushered her hurriedly down the corridor to an examining room where a scrawny old man was lying under a thin blanket on a gurney. His weather-beaten skin was stretched taut over his cheekbones, and his eyes were closed. There was a large purple bruise on his forehead. Margit thought he was unconscious until she noticed the slight flutter of his lips; he seemed to be mumbling softly to himself.

"He was in a car accident, has a mild concussion, but there doesn't seem to be anything else wrong with him," said the nurse. "Didn't break any bones—lucky for him. Made a left turn in front of an oncoming car driven by a teenager who just got her license. She did the smart thing and swerved toward the sidewalk, so she just clipped the rear end of his car and he hit his head on the windshield. Could have been a lot worse. The girl didn't get hurt, but it really shook her up, poor kid. And it wasn't her fault. Anyway, we couldn't find any ID on him except for an expired Danish passport. His name is Søren Rasmussen. We can't understand a word he's saying, so we figured we'd better get an interpreter. Wait here and I'll go find the doctor."

Margit stepped up close to the old man on the bed and said loudly in Danish, "How are you feeling?"

"Who are *you*?" he asked in surprise, his eyes flying open at the sound of the Danish words.

"My name is Margit Andersson, and I'm here to interpret for you. The doctors want to ask you some questions."

"You look just like my niece," he said, putting out a strong, bony hand to pat her arm. "Karin's daughter. She's tall like you. Haven't seen her in twenty years." And the old man's blue eyes welled up with tears. Then he shook his head and snapped, "What do you mean, 'interpret'? What's wrong with these people? Don't they understand plain English? Where am I anyway? How did I get here?"

"You're in Harborview Hospital, Herr Rasmussen. In Seattle. You were in a car accident, and the medics brought you here. And yes, of course they understand English, but you're speaking Danish. That's why I'm here. Is there anyone you'd like me to call? A relative or a friend?"

"*Dansk?*" muttered the old man, putting his left hand up to his forehead and giving Margit a puzzled look.

Just then the doctor came into the room. "So, how are we doing, Mr. Rasmussen?" he asked, trying to sound hearty.

"I'm almost sure he understands English," said Margit. "Do you think the concussion could be making him confused? Could it have crossed the language circuits in his brain somehow?"

"Possibly," replied the weary-looking intern. "But he hasn't responded to any of our questions so far. Let's have you translate them and see if we can get some answers."

After fifteen minutes of back and forth translation, Søren Rasmussen abruptly switched to English, with an occasional Danish phrase thrown in. He was able to tell them that he lived in Ballard, had lived there since 1975, ever since he inherited a house from his brother. He had been on his way to Nielsen's bakery downtown for a cup of coffee and some pastry, and he swore that the light was green at the intersection when he turned left. The doctor finally pronounced him well enough to go home, but warned him to stay in bed for a few days.

"And no more driving," admonished the doctor sternly.

"You didn't even have a license on you. Take the bus or get someone else to drive you. But no more driving for you, my friend. Understand?"

Søren Rasmussen nodded meekly but Margit caught the derogatory "*Satans doktor*" that he muttered under his breath. She decided there was no need to translate.

Margit ended up driving the old man home, since she didn't have the heart to put him in a cab; he probably couldn't afford it. His 1962 Chevy Impala had been towed from the scene of the accident to a local garage, and he would have to get someone to claim it for him later.

Søren's house turned out to be a decrepit one-story rambler with peeling brown paint and a front yard that looked as if it hadn't seen a lawnmower in years—in sharp contrast to the manicured lawns of his neighbors. At the corner of the lot, an ancient plum tree was valiantly putting out blossoms much too early in the season, and a row of scraggly rosebushes with rusty-edged leaves was visible along the side of the house next to the gravel driveway. A wooden boat lay upside down in front of the garage, which was leaning precariously and had a gaping hole in its roof.

Margit helped the old man inside, steering him through the mountains of junk piled up on the living-room floor and into the back bedroom, which was just as cluttered. Stacks of old newspapers and fishing magazines covered the dresser and night-stands. A jumble of fishing tackle, ancient nets, and rain gear was strewn across the floor, and the two overstuffed chairs next to the window were piled high with empty milk cartons. The whole room smelled of sour milk and fish.

Søren sank onto the side of the bed, swung his feet up, and lay back against the grimy pillows. He seemed to be suddenly overcome by the events of the day.

"*Tak*," he said to Margit, "I'm fine now. Thanks for driving me home." His voice was brusque with embarrassment.

"It was nothing," Margit told him in Danish. "Are you sure you're all right? Shall I call one of your neighbors?"

"*Nej tak*," said Søren. "No need to do that. I'm just fine."

"Well, here's my card." Margit handed him an agency card on which she had crossed out the office number and written in her home phone number. "Call me if you need anything. I mean it."

Liisa was always warning the freelancers who handled a lot of court cases not to get personally involved with the "subjects," as she called them. "Remember that you're professionals," she would tell them sternly. "You have to maintain your objectivity. There's no point in getting all mixed up in other people's lives, no matter how tragic their stories might be. If you can't be objective, the judge is going to take you off the case, and that would mean serious trouble for the agency. Keep in mind that *my* reputation is at stake, too."

For the first time Margit fully understood the dilemma of some of her colleagues, when they interpreted for people caught up in immigration cases that were clearly not going to be settled in their favor. It was often hard for the translators to contain their sympathy.

Even though her encounter with Søren Rasmussen did not involve a legal matter (at least not yet, although she wondered whether the parents of the teenage girl would sue Søren for reckless driving), Margit knew it was a breach of agency policy to give out her home number. But she felt sorry for this old man, and he seemed harmless enough. She wished there was something she could do for him.

So when Søren called Margit at home a week later and asked her to translate a letter for him, she had responded with enthusiasm. And when he asked her bluntly, "How much is this gonna cost? I'm not a rich man, you know, and it's just a two-page letter. All you have to do is read it, I just want to know what it says, nothing fancy or anything," Margit did not react with her usual stifled groan.

So many people failed to realize that translating was not a mere reading or typing job. It was a much more complicated process, requiring an intimate knowledge of two cultures as well as two languages. The translator had to be able to comprehend and then convey the subtlest nuances, which were present in even the driest scientific documents. It was meticulous and time-consuming work. And people were almost always shocked at the price.

This time Margit decided to do the translation as a favor. She refused to accept any payment at all—even though this would have infuriated her boss Liisa, had she known about it.

Margit went back to Søren's place several times to read him letters sent by his sister in Århus. It turned out that Søren didn't really need a translator so much as a decoder. His sister's handwriting was that old-fashioned Danish script full of curlicues that took some practice to decipher, and Søren claimed that his eyesight was no longer up to the task. Margit had a sneaking feeling that he just needed company.

So when she got back from New Mexico, Margit was not

surprised to find a message from Søren Rasmussen on her answering machine.

"*Hej Margit, hvordan går det?* Got something here that I need you to translate. Could you come over on Monday morning, about eight o'clock? Should only take a minute and it's important. I've got to put it in the mail right away. *Tak, vi ses.*"

Margit smiled at the raspy voice. That Søren was a feisty old guy. He'd even gone back to driving, much to Margit's horror. But it turned out that he actually did have a valid driver's license; he had just forgotten it at home on the day of the accident. And Søren's insurance company seemed to have smoothed over any litigious squawks from the teenager's parents.

Søren told Margit that the last time his license was up for renewal, he hadn't had any trouble passing the simple vision test—apparently his eyesight was just fine back then. She wished the motor vehicle department had a test for reflexes and attention span too. She shuddered to think of Søren out on the road again, even though he claimed that since the accident he only drove to the senior center half a mile away. For longer excursions, he apparently took the bus.

Margit glanced up at the clock over her desk. Too late to call Søren now. She would just have to drive out to his place before she went in to the agency in the morning and see what it was he needed translated. She didn't really mind the detour—any excuse was welcome if it meant delaying the "discussion" of that salmon translation with Liisa.

⌘

Margit popped out the tape in the middle of Robert Palmer's "Addicted to Love" and parked the Mazda in front of Søren's house. The grass was still knee-deep, and the paint was coming off in big patches around the front windows. All the blinds were drawn, as usual, and the house looked vacant and remote, except that the porch light was flickering on and off. Margit locked her car—even sleepy Ballard had gotten too risky to leave it unlocked these days. She walked briskly up the path to the front door and knocked loudly on the wooden paneling. She knew from her previous visits that the doorbell didn't work.

There was no answer, no sound in the house at all. In spite of Søren's age, his hearing was still sharp, and he usually responded to her knock at once, yanking open the door with a somewhat exasperated, "Goddag, goddag. Kom indenfor."

Margit knocked harder and the door fell away from her touch, opening inward a few inches. There was no entryway; the door led directly into Søren's living room—if it could be called that, since years of accumulated junk had made the space nearly unlivable. Søren spent most of his time in the kitchen, which was actually quite tidy, although it was not exactly what Margit would call spotless.

On her first visit, Margit had been surprised to find bright yellow canisters for flour, sugar, tea, and coffee lined up on the kitchen counter, all labeled neatly in Danish. A little group of spice bottles on the shelf above the stove contained salt, pepper, basil, oregano, nutmeg, cinnamon, and cardamom. Søren's collection of pots and pans hung neatly from a rack over the sink, and a dark green crock on the drainboard held wooden spoons, spatulas, and even a plastic turkey baster.

Margit found it odd that Søren could have such an orderly kitchen while the rest of his place was a disaster zone. And she wondered what on earth he was planning to do with those heaps of milk cartons piled up in his bedroom. When she cautiously asked him whether he had ever considered hiring a housekeeper, he told her sharply that he couldn't afford it, and he didn't need to keep more than one room cleaned up anyway. When she asked him about the milk cartons, he told her that he was saving them for the boat he was going to build for the Green Lake race in the summer.

Margit's colleague, Lars, told her later that old Søren Rasmussen was famous around town for the elaborate contraptions he built for the annual milk-carton derby. One year he even won the prize for the most creative entry: a sleek Viking ship with a dragon's-head prow, ingeniously devised from hundreds of orange-and-white Vitamilk cartons. Unfortunately, the boat lacked the flexibility of its *klinker*-built ancestors, and it sank abruptly in the gentle swell from a passing windsurfer.

A round wooden table painted bright red stood at one end of Søren's kitchen, with a pewter candleholder on top. When Margit came over to read Søren his letters, they would sit at the table and drink strong Ceylon tea, which Margit was startled to see him serve in delicate Royal Copenhagen cups. The man was clearly an original.

An old leather recliner practically filled the alcove next to the kitchen window, which was always covered by a navy-blue curtain. A brass floor lamp with a yellowed paper shade gave Søren enough light to read the morning paper in his recliner, and two bare bulbs in the ceiling fixture lit up the rest of the room.

But today no light was visible under the swinging door

leading into the kitchen when Margit peeked into the dim front room. She called Søren's name. When he didn't answer, she pushed the door all the way open and stepped inside, running her hand over the wall next to the door frame, in search of a light switch. She found the switch and snapped it on.

It took a second for her eyes to adjust to the sudden glare. When she finally focused on the scene before her, it was so improbable that she blinked again, shook her head, and swallowed hard. But the image did not go away—it was real enough.

Søren Rasmussen, dressed in a ragged flannel shirt and a faded pair of overalls, was lying face down in the middle of the floor, his head resting crookedly on a pile of old newspapers. His bare feet were tangled up in a piece of netting, his left hand was stretched out toward the sagging sofa, as if he meant to pull himself up, and his right arm was bent under his chest. In the middle of his back the hilt of a knife protruded obscenely from a dark brown splotch of dried blood.

"Oh my God," whispered Margit, putting her hand up to her mouth. "Oh my God."

Then she whirled around, ran out the door, and raced down the front walk to her car. Frantically she dug the keys out of her handbag and unlocked the door. She sank into the driver's seat and picked up the car phone, which she had bought only a few weeks ago, deciding it was a necessity if she was going to keep driving her old Mazda around at night. She dialed 911.

"There's a knife," she gasped, "and he's dead!" She managed to give the operator the address, promising to stay there until the police arrived. Then she switched off the phone, propped her elbows on the steering wheel, and buried her face in her hands.

2

Here, drink this," said Renny, setting a double espresso in front of Margit and sitting down across from her at a corner table in the Cedar Café in West Seattle.

Renny's answer to any crisis was a strong cup of coffee, even though she could no longer drink it herself. The sudden onset of Menière's syndrome a few years back had cured Renny of her caffeine addiction for good. The reeling vertigo characteristic of that disease of the inner ear was aggravated by salt, tobacco smoke, and caffeine. All three had been among Renny's favorite vices, but she decided that none of them was worth the nauseating seasickness that could force her to the floor, clutching her head as the room whirled past in a blur of colors. Even decaf brews made her dizzy, so she had to settle for the bland substitute of herbal teas.

"But there's no harm in sniffing the stuff," Renny would say with a laugh, inhaling the earthy aroma of the Guatemalan blend as she turned on the grinder for the umpteenth time during her shift behind the counter. And the regulars at the Cedar

Café all claimed that Renny made the best lattes in town—no small compliment in a city rampant with coffee connoisseurs.

"What did the police say?" she asked Margit as she patted her friend's hand.

"Not much," said Margit, taking a sip of the murky coffee and shuddering at the powerful taste. "They asked me a lot of questions about why I was there and how I knew Søren and whether I touched anything. I told them that I barely stepped inside the door. The detective in charge seemed disgusted with the state of Søren's house. He said it was going to be a miracle if they found fingerprints or any other evidence in all that mess.

"After they took my statement, they finally said I could leave. I drove over to the agency, but I guess I must have looked pretty pale, because even Liisa could see that something was wrong. When I told everybody what happened, Liisa said she wouldn't need me until tomorrow and told me to go home. Jennifer prescribed ginseng tea, and Yuri started raving about the Russian mafia knocking off innocent citizens in Ballard."

"You've got to be kidding," said Renny.

"No, really, it's his latest obsession. He swears that these *nouveau* gangsters are going to take over the world. He says they're a bigger threat than the arms race ever was. He's always so extreme. And Lars volunteered to fix the problems in that salmon translation I did before I left on vacation—Liisa was quibbling about my word choice again. That Lars is such a sweetheart."

Margit leaned back in her chair and gave her friend a bleak look. "God, I feel terrible. Poor Søren! Who would want to hurt an old coot like that?"

"It seems so incredible," said Renny, shaking her head. "Did he ever talk about any enemies he had? Or old lovers who were still holding a grudge because he jilted them back when he was a dapper young Dane in the old country?"

Margit shook her head with a smile. She found it hard to imagine Søren's gaunt frame wrapped in a passionate embrace, even in his younger days. He seemed like such an ornery guy, and a real loner.

"What did those letters from his sister say, anyway?" Renny went on. "Anything in them that might be a clue?"

She loved mysteries and was a big fan of Dorothy Sayers, Josephine Tey, and P. D. James. Her latest discovery was *Blanche on the Lam* by Barbara Neely. But she didn't have much patience for high-tech thrillers. "Too much blood and gore, too much hardware," she always complained. "Give me a good psychological drama, something a little twisted but not too perverse." And it was Renny's sense for the offbeat and the slightly sinister side of human nature, combined with an extravagant imagination, that made her such a good painter. Her latest works were veiled nudes, which all had an extra appendage of one sort or another.

Margit's reading preferences usually tended toward 19th-century classics, but she had actually translated a few Swedish suspense novels and found it amusing to unravel the clues. Curiosity and tenacity were essential in her line of work and, like any skilled translator, she was a good detective. But she liked solving real mysteries, not the fictional kind. She loved to delve into her reference books for the story of an obscure 13th-century monk who was mentioned in an article she was translating. Or she would happily spend half an hour tracking down the correct name for a minuscule component in a calibration instrument. She was adept at research, and her personal collection of reference books was worthy of any good public library.

"The letters to Søren were perfectly ordinary ones," said Margit. "Family news, that type of thing. His sister Karin was trying to get him to come over for a visit, and she seemed really adamant about it. It sounded urgent, but she didn't say why. Søren told me that he hadn't been back to Denmark in twenty years, not since he first came over here when he inherited the house in Ballard from his brother. He wasn't keen on going back either. Said he couldn't afford it, and didn't see any use in making such a long trip. Everybody he used to know was dead anyway. Søren joked about his sister wanting to see him so urgently—said she was getting sentimental in her old age."

Margit took another sip of espresso.

"I thought she must be ancient because her handwriting was so cramped and shaky, but Søren said she was eight years younger than him. I wonder if she'll come over here for the funeral. I told the police that as far as I know, she and her daughter are Søren's only relatives."

"That poor old guy," said Renny, shaking her head. "The murderer will probably turn out to be some fourteen-year-old kid who was looking for money to buy drugs and panicked when Søren caught him prowling around in his house. But it does seem odd that he would use a knife instead of a gun— everybody seems to have guns these days, especially the kids."

Renny threw a glance over her shoulder and said, "Listen, I've got to get back to work. Bob's giving me the eye. He's a great cook, but the customers don't think much of his barista skills, and he knows it. I'd better go. You take it easy, Margit.

Treat yourself to a hot bath or take a long walk in the park. Do something nice for yourself today. You've had a bad shock. And call me tonight. I'm going to an opening at the Douglas Gallery, but I'll be home after nine. We'll talk."

Renny stood up and went around the table to give Margit a quick hug. Then she picked up her teacup and headed toward the front of the café, where five or six customers were impatiently calling out orders to a harried and scowling Bob.

Margit downed the last drops of her espresso, glad that she had stopped by the café to see her friend. The early morning scene at Søren's house, with the hubbub of detectives and medics, the questions, and the stern warning that the police would be in touch with her, had upset Margit more than she thought. By the time she had left the translation agency and turned south onto the viaduct to drive home, she was feeling thoroughly disoriented. When she finally got off the West Seattle bridge, she had to pull into the Safeway parking lot in the Admiral district because she was shaking so badly. Ten minutes of deep breathing had finally steadied her nerves. Now that she had talked to Renny, she felt almost normal again.

Margit left the café with a wave to her friend and drove home. Gregor was curled up in his favorite spot under the spruce in the back yard, but the sound of the Mazda in the driveway brought him out of his nest. He rushed to beat Margit to the front door and then stood there complaining while she looked for her key.

When she pushed open the door, Gregor squirmed inside, jumping lightly over a white envelope lying on the floor. Margit picked it up with surprise. Mail was hardly ever delivered to her house anymore, now that she had a post office box. Ads for housecleaning and lawnmowing services and pizza coupons addressed to "Occupant" were about the only things that came through her mail slot these days. But this was a real letter, although she noticed there was no return address.

Margit put her bag and briefcase on the dining-room table and sat down before she slit open the envelope. There were two sheets of paper inside. One of them was a poor photocopy of what looked like a runic verse. The other was a pencil sketch of three tiny, stylized figures. She turned the papers over, but there was no message, and the envelope held no clue either. Her name and street address were scrawled in black ink on the front, and the postmark was too blurry to read.

Margit was mystified and also slightly annoyed. Really, this was all too much for one day. And she hadn't gotten enough sleep either—her old nightmares were back, after a week-long reprieve while she was in New Mexico. She hardly ever had nightmares when she traveled, and besides, Joe's company in bed had left her both too exhausted and too content to be bothered by bad dreams. Not for the first time, she wished that they lived in the same town. She loved Joe, but this long-distance romancing was beginning to wear thin.

She wanted him home at the end of the day. She wanted to sit in the kitchen and watch him chopping up the tomatoes and onions for his vegetarian lasagna as she sipped a glass of Chianti. She wanted to wake up in the morning and find him stretched out beside her, the sunlight giving a reddish gleam to his curly brown hair. And then she would laugh at his grumbling when she told him it was late and he had to get up.

But they had known each other for over a year now, and neither one showed any willingness to pick up everything and move. Joe Niehoff was a sculptor whose growing reputation as a Southwest artist was beginning to attract wealthy collectors, thanks largely to Mrs. Herbert McKenzie, a Santa Fe arts enthusiast who had taken Joe under her ample wing. She was constantly bringing her rich friends over to his studio to "have a look." Margit took an instant dislike to Mrs. McKenzie and always found some urgent reason to make her getaway if "the Matron," as Margit called her, showed up at Joe's studio when she was there.

Joe had spent the first thirty years of his life in Ohio (a fact that he concealed from most people), but he had been in Santa Fe for nearly two decades now, and he considered himself a New Mexican. He liked the wide-open landscape, and he needed plenty of space for his monumental iron figures that seemed to shoulder their way up out of the ground. He couldn't imagine living anywhere else.

Margit, on the other hand, could picture herself moving away from the Northwest someday. She could even see herself living in an old, but beautifully renovated, adobe house filled with pottery and hand-woven rugs. But there was no work for her in Santa Fe, and she was not convinced that Liisa would be willing to send jobs to her long-distance. In this age of computers and telecommunications, there was really no reason for her to be in the same town as the agency. But Liisa liked to keep a tight rein on her freelancers, and Margit assumed that she would soon be replaced if she moved too far away.

That was the rational reason for her reluctance to pull up roots and move to the Southwest. That was what she told Renny and her other Seattle friends. But to herself she had to admit that she was simply too unsure of her relationship with Joe. And she wanted him to make the first move, she wanted *him* to give up something for *her*, and not the other way around.

Margit sighed. What a day. She was feeling bad enough already about Søren's death—she didn't need to get stuck in the quagmire of the whole "commitment" issue right now. Stop it, she told herself, think about something else.

She looked down at the pieces of paper in her hand. The three lines of runes were indecipherable. Years ago Margit had spent a short time studying runic inscriptions when she was taking a class in Old Norse, a requirement for her degree in Scandinavian languages. But she was disappointed to find that most runes were no more revealing than modern-day graffiti, a mere recording of who had passed through, who had died on that spot, or who had stopped to carve his name. And all those sagas full of sword-brandishing avengers, whacked-off limbs, and ancient curses had actually put her to sleep. She had never cared much for boys' adventure stories, anyway. So after she passed the final exam, she put away her Old Norse books for good. She would need an expert to tell her what these runes said.

But there was something familiar about the three figures sketched on the other sheet of paper: a bird that bore an uncanny resemblance to Heckel and Jeckel pecking at a recumbent fish; a three-headed man clutching a club in one hand and some kind of goat or sheep in the other; and a woman wildly dancing, her hair flung out around her like a swirling cape. Margit had seen these figures somewhere before—she was sure of it.

She stood up and went through the kitchen with Gregor sauntering after her. She snapped on the light switch on the far wall and opened the door to the steep flight of stairs leading down to the basement. This was another reason why she would find it hard to move away. When the realtor first showed her this house, Margit was unimpressed with the clumsy, boxy exterior and the small rooms on the main floor. The sparkle ceilings were another strike against the place. But one look at the spacious basement with the fireplace at one end, and Margit decided to buy the house. She had always dreamed of having her own library, and the two huge rooms were exactly what she needed.

As soon as Margit moved in, she hired a carpenter to build her dozens of floor-to-ceiling bookshelves, and then she brought in an electrician to install rows of track lighting. Now she had her own stacks in the basement, just like in a real library. Finally she could unpack all her boxes of books and arrange the volumes systematically on the shelves; finally she could find what she needed when her translating called for a particular reference work. And best of all, there was plenty of room for more books—a fact that encouraged her frequent bookstore visits.

Margit switched on lights at the end of each row and then headed down one aisle toward the history section. She pulled out a couple of hefty volumes and blew the dust off the tops. Then she bent down and scanned the lower shelves until she found another book she was looking for. She carried all of them over to the couch in front of the fireplace and sat down in the circle of light from the green-shaded lamp on the end table. Gregor jumped up onto the opposite armrest and settled down in a meatloaf position, his eyes closed and his throat rumbling contentedly.

Margit opened the first book, *The Nordic Past*, and squinted at the table of contents, leaning back a little farther against the cushions to put more distance between her eyes and the tiny print on the page. Her vision was really getting bad lately; she was going to have to get reading glasses one of these days.

There were sections on sacrificial rites, grave goods, pottery sherds, leathery-skinned bog people, and Viking raids, as well as several chapters on rune stones in both Sweden and Denmark. But Margit didn't have the patience to read through the tedious text right now. She was looking for a photo or an illustration that she vaguely remembered seeing a few years back when she was translating a doctoral thesis for an archaeology student at Lund University. She riffled through the pages but found nothing useful.

Margit closed the thick tome and put it down next to her. Then she picked up the slim volume that she had pulled from the lower shelf—a book in Danish that had been published several years ago in honor of the Queen's fiftieth birthday. Margit laughed to herself and hoped that when she reached the half-century mark, her friends would have better sense than to give her a work entitled *The Face of Antiquity*. She let the book fall open in her lap and then squawked so loudly that Gregor's head snapped around toward her, his eyes widening in surprise.

There it was—a photograph of a centuries-old sketch showing snakes, centaurs, deer, sword-wielding men, and two figures that matched the ones on her piece of paper: a bird pecking at a fish and a three-headed man holding a club in one hand and a goat in the other. Only the dancing woman seemed to be missing. Margit was looking at the images engraved and embossed on the famous Golden Horns—two priceless 5th-century drinking horns that disappeared in 1802.

She hurriedly read through the text and then closed the

book with a sigh, still thoroughly mystified. Why would someone send her this drawing? Why the anonymous envelope and
mysterious runes? And why was someone so interested in the
Golden Horns?

3

When Margit walked into the Koivisto Translation Agency in Belltown at ten o'clock the following morning, she was not in the best of moods. Her regular nightmares had been replaced by visions of tiny figures swarming up over the bed, crawling under the quilt, and creeping along her bare skin. She woke up at six a.m., shivering, her nightgown soaked with sweat. She was filled with loathing. It took forty minutes on the Nordic Track and then a long hot shower to rid her skin of a prickling sensation that invisible creatures were still marching along her limbs.

"Bad night?" asked Lars cautiously, taking note of Margit's frazzled appearance as she plunked her briefcase onto a desk in a corner of the communal office used by the agency's freelancers.

There were five battered wooden desks in the room, each with a dull-red lamp clamped onto the edge, and a PC, a small laser printer, and a copy stand on top. Faded travel posters were taped up over the desks, and the far wall was entirely covered by a giant map of the world from the National Geographic Society (several years old, since the pink of the Soviet Union still encompassed the Baltics, and the brown of the DDR had not yet merged with the green of West Germany). A threadbare gray carpet blotchy with years of accumulated stains, a wooden coat tree missing some of its pegs, and five cheap desk chairs with burnt orange fabric covering the seats completed the decor. The office always seemed a little musty and smelled faintly of cigarette smoke, even though they had all agreed on a no-smoking policy long ago. Liisa had spared no expense on the computer equipment, but otherwise the room was less than inviting.

Freelancers never worked more than twenty hours a week in the office anyway, since that was the legal limit for them to be on-site. And Liisa claimed there wasn't enough work to keep more than a couple of translators and editors on staff, even part-time. Margit didn't really pay much attention to the freelancers' room because she did most of her work at home.

The front half of the agency, however, was tastefully furnished with sleek leather sofas and chairs, glass coffee tables, and Danish-design lamps. And the agency's enormous library had an impressive collection of all the latest dictionaries, encyclopedias, and specialized reference works in a multitude of languages. But Liisa saw no reason to waste money on decorating the translators' cubbyhole, since clients never got beyond the front offices.

Lars was perched on a balance chair at the desk next to the only window in the room. It was the choice position, and he always tried to get in early enough to claim it on the days he decided to work in the office. This was usually no problem for a morning person like Lars; he did his best work between six a.m. and noon.

"Bad night is right," said Margit with a wan smile. "You

wouldn't even believe it." She sat down at the desk and switched on the lamp.

"Still thinking about poor old Søren?" asked Lars sympathetically, rolling his chair back and turning it around so he could face Margit. "What a shock. I used to see him at the milk carton races every year, launching another one of his loony contraptions at Green Lake. Everybody else came with teams of people, but old Søren would get a couple of bystanders to help him unload his boat from a beat-up truck he had borrowed, and then he would sail off alone.

"And once I saw him at the Valhalla tavern when I took Derek there as a joke. I told Derek that if he was going to live with me, he would have to get used to all the Scandihoovian stuff, so I dragged him along to the Valhalla to listen to the old-timers speaking their Swenglish—it just cracks me up. Anyway, when we sat down at the bar, I noticed Søren at the other end. He was waving his arms around and telling his buddies some story, but I couldn't catch what it was about.

"He was a funny old guy, but completely harmless. I can't imagine why anyone would want to stab him to death."

Margit inhaled sharply, seeing once again Søren's lifeless form sprawled across the junk on his living-room floor. She jabbed at the power button on the computer and scowled furiously as the opening sequences scrolled through the memory tests and virus scan.

She wanted to pull out that bloody knife and hurl it out the front window of his house with all her might. She wanted to yank Søren to his feet and tell him to stop playing around, she didn't like his game. She wanted to give him a good hard shake and yell in his ear, "You can't be dead!"

"Margit? Are you OK?" Lars was suddenly standing next

to her, his hand on her shoulder, a look of concern on his face. "Yeah," she murmured, looking up briefly. "I'm OK. Thanks. It just makes me so mad."

Lars squeezed her shoulder gently and said, "Me too." Then he went back to his desk and sat down, peering at his computer screen through his wire-rimmed glasses, his straw-blond hair falling boyishly over his forehead.

"Lars?" said Margit after a few minutes in which the only sound in the room was the clacking of the two keyboards. "Do you know anything about the Golden Horns?"

"The Golden Horns found in Denmark?" asked Lars, turning his head toward her. "Weren't they stolen or something?"

"Yes," said Margit, "that's right. But the really extraordinary thing about them was how they were found. I was reading about them last night. The first one was discovered in a field by a young girl in 1639. Kirsten Svendsdatter was her name, a lacemaker from Østerby, not far from Tønder. She literally stumbled on this incredible, heavy gold horn with elaborate figures stamped and embossed on the outside. It was thought to be a drinking horn from the 5th century. Eventually the horn ended up with King Christian IV, and it was put in the Royal Art Chamber.

"Then almost a century later, in 1734, a second horn was found. And the weird thing was that it turned up in the exact same field, near Gallehus in South Jutland. This time a farmer named Erich Lassen found it while he was doing his plowing. It was heavier than the first one, even though it was missing one end. And in addition to all the engraved figures, it had a runic inscription on it giving the name of the artist: Lægæst, son of Holti. The second horn came into the possession of the monarchy too—King Christian VI this time, and he put it in the royal art collection along with the first one."

"And that's where they were stolen from?" asked Lars.

"Yes," said Margit. "In 1802, by a really unscrupulous guy. A goldsmith and counterfeiter named Niels Heidenreich. He made himself a duplicate key to the Royal Art Chamber and waltzed right in and stole the Golden Horns. He got caught, of course, but not before he had melted down the ancient treasures in his kitchen. It was a terrible loss."

"Greed triumphs over art once again. The age-old story," said Lars with a shake of his head.

"Exactly," replied Margit. "But these horns were more than just works of art, they became symbols for Denmark itself. Oehlenschlæger even wrote a famous poem about them."

"Why are you so interested in all of this stuff right now? I thought Liisa was giving you a rush Norwegian job about refrigeration systems to translate. Don't tell me you got some great archaeological treatise to work on instead. And here I am, stuck with this endless computer manual."

"Don't worry," said Margit with a laugh, "you got the better deal. This job she gave me is going to be a real bear. It's a bunch of legal documents about some big shake-up in the refrigeration industry—just your cup of tea.

"But listen, this is the strange part," she continued. "I got this letter yesterday with a sketch of three figures and two of them are almost identical to . . ."

"Margit! Good—you're here," Liisa practically shouted as she rushed into the room, coming to an abrupt stop a few feet from Margit's desk. She was always in a hurry. "Feeling better? You look much better. Did you find the Norfridge file I left in your box? They need it by five, they're sending a courier. Now, about that salmon job that Lars edited for you, I still think there are some rough spots, and maybe you'd better have another look at it before we send it out. Do that after the Norfridge job. Can you get to it today? We've had it way too long and the client's getting antsy. OK? Good." And with a brisk "Morning, Lars!" Liisa swept out of the room.

"Somebody needs to cut down on her caffeine intake," mumbled Margit, wondering again how a woman in such a rush could always manage to look so classy. Liisa was a great believer in "power dressing," and today she was wearing a cobalt-blue suit that brought out the piercing blue of her eyes. Her hair was cut fashionably short, and she was wearing her silver Kalevala Koru jewelry. Margit glanced down at her own limp cotton dress. It was her favorite and she had specifically put it on that morning to cheer herself up, but it clearly could not compete with Liisa's stylish attire. There was no use even trying.

Margit turned back to her work with a sigh, thinking in despair about that stupid salmon translation. It was turning into the job from hell—she just couldn't seem to get rid of it. And the worst thing of all was that she was losing money. She got paid by the word, not by the hour, so all this extra time spent editing and revising was at her own expense. She'd give it one more look, no more than an hour, and that was *it*. If Liisa still wasn't satisfied, she'd just have to fix it herself. What a perfectionist. She drove everybody crazy. But she did bring in steady work from a long list of corporate clients—Margit had to give her credit for that. Liisa knew how to keep the agency's customers happy.

The phone was ringing and Margit got up to answer it. There was only one phone in the room, sitting on top of an old

American Heritage dictionary on a rickety typewriter stand to the left of the doorway. It was not a direct line. Hannah, the receptionist, put through calls to the freelancers from the front office.

"Margit Andersson," she said crisply, impatient to get back to her work.

"Miss Andersson? This is Detective Tristano of the Seattle Police Department. I'm working on the Rasmussen case, and we've found something you might be able to help us with. Looks like some kind of letter, could be Danish. If we fax a copy over to you, do you think you could translate it?"

"Oh . . . sure," said Margit, "send it over. But I'm afraid I won't be able to get to it until tonight, I'm in the middle of a rush job. Is that OK?"

"No problem," the detective assured Margit, so she gave him the agency's fax number.

"Trouble?" asked Lars, looking over his shoulder and seeing Margit frown as she put down the phone.

"The police," she told him. "They found something they want me to translate. Something to do with Søren."

And then she went back to her desk and forced herself to concentrate on the Norfridge job, meticulously plodding through page after page of the documents clipped to her copy stand. She couldn't waste any more time if she was going to get it done by five.

Lars turned off his computer and straightened the papers on his desk. He was going to meet Derek for lunch. It was only eleven o'clock, but he had already put in four hours, and his muscles were feeling cramped from sitting so long. On the days when he worked at the agency, he always walked the twelve blocks to Derek's office in the Dexter Horton building, no matter what the weather. Today the sky was gray again, the Olympics had disappeared behind a veil of fog, and Mt. Rainier had vanished from the horizon. The forecast called for rain, but Seattleites rarely changed their plans because of inclement weather. Lars got up and strode across the room with his typically buoyant step. He grabbed his leather jacket from the coat tree and then called out *"Hej då"* to Margit as he left the office.

Neither Margit nor Lars gave any more thought to the murder investigation or the Golden Horns.

⌘

At seven o'clock that evening Margit switched off the computer and leaned back in her chair, putting her right hand up to her left shoulder and massaging the tight muscles. She yawned loudly, glad to have the office to herself finally, after a long day. At least she had finished both jobs on time, and to Liisa's satisfaction, which was always a miracle.

Yuri had been in the office that afternoon, and he could be a real distraction, since he tended to rant at the screen while he worked. He would complain about the idiotic content of whatever he was translating, or sneer at the poor grammar and inconsistent logic. His tirades had gotten particularly bad lately, ever since Liisa had landed a big client: the Sound Evangelical Church, which was hoping to convert thousands of Russians to their faith by showering the newly liberated throngs with religious tracts. And of course all the literature had to be translated into Russian, so Yuri had plenty of work. But he was not a man who suffered zealots gladly, and he let everyone know it. His antidote was to listen to Heavy Metal while he worked. Margit was always relieved to see Yuri clap the headset of his Walkman over his shaggy mop of black hair after half an hour of vociferous activity.

Margit pulled a brush out of the side pocket of her briefcase and gave her straight, shoulder-length hair a few swift strokes. Then she touched up her lipstick, staring at her dim reflection in the blank computer screen. She had her father's long nose and large mouth, but her mother's high cheekbones and thin face.

OK, she said to herself, time to go. Gregor was going to be mad if he didn't get fed pretty soon, and she was hungry too. The veggie sandwich and apple that she'd brought with her for lunch seemed light-years ago, and she could already feel the first signs of low blood sugar. She would start getting cranky if she didn't have some food soon. She popped a peppermint LifeSaver into her mouth and made herself imagine the big plate of pasta she was going to cook for dinner, topped with olive oil, Italian tomatoes, mushrooms, artichoke hearts, and lots of garlic. She decided to stop at the Co-op on her way home to buy some bread and a bottle of chardonnay.

Margit picked up the heavy red Norwegian-English dictionary, the thick *Glossary of Legal Terms*, and the thesaurus that she had been using all day, and cradled them in her left arm. She would put them back in the library on her way out. She hated it when other translators left their reference books lying around. Who did they think was going to pick up after them, anyway?

Jennifer was the worst offender. Her desk was always covered with stacks of Chinese dictionaries, and when she ran out of space, she piled them on the floor. She also wrote herself notes on little stick-on flags and plastered them all around the edge of her monitor. She often ate lunch at her desk, and the styrofoam containers of leftover noodles and rice swimming in a pool of soy sauce would still be there at the end of the day. Whoever came along after her had to spend twenty minutes hauling away the books and cleaning up everything before the desk was in usable condition. Jennifer kept promising to reform, but after a few days of exemplary neatness, she would always fall back into her old habits.

With her right hand Margit switched off the desk lamp, slung the strap of her bag over her shoulder, and then grabbed the handles of her briefcase. The light from the hall filled the doorway, casting a wedge of yellow across the dingy gray carpet. She took two steps toward the door, and that's when she heard the sound. A muffled thud from somewhere in the front offices.

Everyone else had gone for the day. Even Liisa had left at 6:30, stopping in to say goodbye before she raced off to a dinner meeting with executives from MjukSystemen, a new Swedish software company that was looking for an American translation agency to help launch its products in the States. Liisa had gone to school with the president's cousin, and she was never shy about using even the most distant connection to land a client. She was a fierce competitor and had managed to snag quite a few major accounts that normally would have fallen to some big New York agency.

Before she left, Liisa had tossed a folder onto Margit's desk. "More stuff from Thor Cheese," she said, "but you can take it home with you, it's not due till Friday. And there's a fax in there for you. From the police." Then she had waved and dashed out the door.

Margit shifted the heavy reference books in her left arm and took a tighter grip on her briefcase. She must be hearing things. God, she was jumpy lately.

Then she heard the sound again, quite clearly this time.

Someone was moving around in the front office. She could hear footsteps on the hardwood floor, which tended to creak, especially in the corner near the receptionist's desk.

Margit quickly stepped back, out of the light from the doorway, and held her breath. She could feel the sweat trickling down her sides and the heat rising up in her face. Maybe it was one of her colleagues, maybe somebody forgot something and came back to get it. Margit inched her way over to the wall, still carrying her books, shoulder bag, and briefcase, afraid that if she put anything down she would make too much noise. She peered cautiously around the door frame and down the long hall.

Then she saw him. A thin figure wearing a dark turtleneck and black pants was bending over one of the low file cabinets lining the hall. But it was the brown leather gloves that sent a chill down her spine. This was definitely not one of the translators. Only somebody up to no good would be wearing gloves indoors.

Margit's eyes fell on the blocky outline of the phone sitting on the typewriter stand on the other side of the doorway, but she didn't dare risk crossing through the swath of light. What the hell am I going to do? she thought. Her heart was thundering, her pulse roaring, her lungs straining.

She glanced back down the hallway and was appalled to

see the dark-clad man straighten up, and then move to the next file cabinet. He was coming closer. It was only a matter of time before he would reach the cabinet right outside the door of the freelancers' office. If he decided to enter the room itself, she would have nowhere to hide.

Margit's eyes darted around the dim room, skimming over the shadowy shapes of the furniture, and came to rest on the one window in the office. It was sealed shut, of course, since the building had been designed for air conditioning, not fresh air. In a split second Margit made up her mind.

She backed away from the door, tiptoed to the middle of the room, and carefully set her briefcase and shoulder bag on the floor. Then she took hold of the three heavy reference books with both hands, raised them high over her head, and pitched them as hard as she could at the windowpane.

The sound of splintering glass was as piercing as a flash of lightning.

In one swift movement Margit scooped up her belongings and raced across the room, madly slamming her briefcase along the edge of the window frame to knock out jagged points of glass. Then she heaved both bags outside. Frantically, she flung her right leg over the windowsill, ducked her head, pulled her left leg over, and with an involuntary shriek she dropped over the side.

4

O w!" moaned Margit, wincing as she bent down to pick up a book.

"Hey, let me do that," said Renny. "Stop moving around so much. Girl, you look like shit. It's a good thing your office is only on the second floor, or you could be lying in the hospital right now with your legs in traction, instead of hobbling around with a few bruises and some stitches in your butt."

"This is bad enough, believe me," said Margit with a grimace, moving aside so Renny could put the computer keyboard on top of a tall stack of encyclopedias.

Gregor hovered around anxiously at their feet. He could tell that something was wrong with Margit, and he was always uneasy if his furniture got moved—he hated any kind of change.

They had already taken the ergonomic desk chair out of the room and lifted the computer monitor onto a footstool placed on top of Margit's desk. Now she was all set to work standing up. She had called Renny half an hour earlier and told her that she needed help rigging up her computer because she couldn't sit down.

"What do you mean you can't sit down?" asked her friend.

"I had a little accident last night," said Margit, and then she told Renny about the intruder and her leap out the window.

An elderly woman who lived in one of those new high-rises in Belltown had seen Margit come crashing out of the office window into the bushes below and called the police. Before she knew it, Margit was confronted by three tense officers, pistols drawn, yelling at her to freeze and put her hands in the air. In her dazed state, she was not entirely coherent, and it took a lot of explaining to convince the police that she was the victim, not the perpetrator. They finally got Liisa on her beeper, and she came over to identify her employee. Margit wasn't sure what made her boss more furious—the break-in or the interruption of her negotiations over dinner.

The police made a thorough search of the office. The lock on the door had been jimmied and one of the hall file cabinets was open, but nothing seemed to be missing.

Liisa called a security company to watch the office for the rest of the night. She was fuming over the ease with which the intruder had broken into the agency. Obviously the burglar alarm on the front door of the building was malfunctioning, and she was going to have to install more security in the office itself. She was already worrying about the expense.

Then Liisa insisted on driving Margit over to Swedish Hospital in spite of her protests that she was just fine. Margit had stubbornly refused the offer of medical assistance from the police, but her boss wouldn't take no for an answer.

"Oh sure," said Liisa sarcastically. "You really look just fine. Come on, get in the car."

Margit had several cuts on her hands, but nothing serious,

although her fingers were puffy and stiff the next morning. Thank God she'd still be able to type. But the backs of her legs were badly scratched, and one cut in a strategic position required ten stitches. That's why she couldn't sit down.

Renny came right over when Margit called her at nine the next morning. She lived only a block away. As she followed her groaning friend into the study, she couldn't help teasing her a little.

"Geez, Margit, a few minor abrasions and contusions shouldn't slow you down like this. In all those Dick Francis books, the hero falls off his horse, suffers multiple injuries, and gets clobbered by a spanner, but he's back at the racetrack the very next day."

"Thanks a lot," said Margit sourly. "I bet he isn't forty years old, with a bad back and a sedentary lifestyle. My whole body is black and blue, I got about three hours sleep, and my head is killing me. This *would* have to happen on the one day that I wear a dress to work. From now on, it's back to jeans and a t-shirt."

"And steel-plated underwear," added Renny, finally making Margit laugh.

After they finished rearranging the computer, Margit offered Renny a cup of tea. They went into the kitchen, and while they sipped their Orange Zinger, Margit brought out the runes and sketches and told her friend what she knew about the Golden Horns.

"Too weird," said Renny. "So what does all this have to do with Søren?"

"I don't know," said Margit gloomily, "I really don't know."

Renny glanced up at the kitchen clock, gulped the last of her tea, and gave Margit a quick hug. "Gotta run, kiddo. Bob's expecting me at work in ten minutes. Sorry I haven't been home the last two nights when you called. Preston showed up at that opening at the Douglas Gallery, and you know what I'm like when he's in town. Head over heels and crazy with hormones."

"Why don't you marry him, Renny?"

"Oh God, no. He'd make a lousy husband, and I'd be an even worse wife. The daily grind would turn us into a couple of screaming banshees. This way, we're always glad to see each other, if you know what I mean. And he had this great suite at the Alexis with satin sheets and terrycloth bathrobes. It was heaven."

Preston Fairchild was an art dealer from L.A. who had discovered Renny's work at a group show in Bellevue a couple of years back. He liked what he saw and went over to her studio to look at more of her paintings. They'd been having a steamy, if intermittent, affair ever since.

Margit thought it ironic that both she and Renny had ended up with long-distance lovers. Maybe it was because each of them had already been through one failed marriage, and at their age they were not about to plunge precipitously into another.

"See ya," yelled Renny as she ran out the door, with Gregor right behind her. He never failed to take advantage of an available exit—closed doors were the bane of every cat's existence.

Margit sighed and went back to her study, taking out a Doobie Brothers CD from the rack and slipping it into the player. She listened to the opening lines of "The Doctor," turned up the volume a notch, and then pulled the Thor Cheese job out of her briefcase. She liked to listen to tunes while she worked, and the more boring the translation, the more raucous her choice of music. Today her throbbing head made her select something in the mid-raucous range. Maybe work would distract her from her aching joints. She opened the folder and a page sailed out, landing at her feet. Margit leaned down with a groan and picked it up. The oval stamp at the top of the page said "Seattle Police Department"—she'd forgotten all about the fax from the police.

⌘

Ten minutes later, Margit whistled sharply in amazement as she typed the last word on the screen. The fax clipped to the holder on the side of her monitor fluttered in the light breeze coming through the open window. Margit glanced to her left and noticed that the sun was trying to break through the clouds, and she could see tiny green buds on the cherry tree in the back yard. Spring actually seemed to be on its way after all. Two teenage girls walked past, dressed in tank tops and shorts. At the first sign of sunshine, Seattleites whipped out their summer clothes, even if the temperature was still only 55 degrees.

The fax from the police turned out to be a letter written in Danish, as the detective had surmised, but a most peculiar one.

There was no date, but the letter was addressed to Mr. Harry Karovsky at the law firm of Samuel, Aitkins, Wilson, and Karovsky, 1485 Fourth Avenue, Suite 801, Seattle.

Dear Mr. Karovsky,

Excuse me for bothering you. I know you must be a busy man. I don't want to take up too much of your time. You probably don't remember me. I was the one who took you on that fishing trip up to Point No Point a couple of years ago. You caught two salmon but your friend didn't catch any. We stopped to eat sandwiches for lunch. I was sitting in the other end of the boat but I couldn't help overhearing what you said. I'm sorry to tell you that I eavesdropped. That's why I'm writing this letter to you today. Please excuse me.

Your friend said you shouldn't take a case if a person couldn't pay. He said you were nuts to do so much work for nothing. He said your company didn't need to do charity cases.

You said you didn't go to law school just to make money. You said you wanted to right a wrong if you could. You said sometimes that was more important than money. I only have five hundred dollars in my savings account. I know it's not enough but I'll give you all my money if you will help me. Please call me as soon as possible if you think you can help me. Excuse me for bothering you.

Sincerely,

Søren Rasmussen

Margit was struck by the mixture of deference and barely suppressed desperation in Søren's letter. He obviously hadn't trusted his English enough to compose a letter to a lawyer, so he had written it out in Danish. This must be what he had wanted Margit to translate—and why the letter was so vague. Søren knew she would be reading it, and he didn't want to reveal too much about something that was none of her business.

The letter was written in a scrawling, sloppy script, filling almost the entire sheet of paper, and it took some effort to decipher all of the words correctly. But what astounded Margit most was the familiarity of the messy handwriting.

It matched exactly the hasty cursive script on the envelope that had arrived at Margit's house on the day she discovered the murder. The runes and drawings had come from Søren.

⌘

"Thank you, Miss Andersson. You've been most helpful," said Detective Tristano a little too politely as Margit finished reading Søren's letter to him over the phone. "Would you mind faxing your translation to us?"

"OK, I'll send it right over." Margit's home office was equipped with a fax, modem, laser printer, and CD-ROM player—all essential items for a freelance translator. And she had recently bought herself a new Pentium.

"I hear you were mixed up in a little trouble last night," continued the detective.

"Somebody broke into the agency I work for," said Margit defensively. She didn't appreciate the implied accusation. "It had nothing to do with me. I just happened to be working late."

"I see," said Detective Tristano, annoying Margit further. Did he think she made a habit of being interrogated by the police? And twice in one week, at that?

"Are you going to call this lawyer?" she asked abruptly.

There was a slight hesitation before the detective replied. Margit assumed he was trying to gauge exactly how much to tell her.

"We contacted Mr. Karovsky as soon as we saw his name on the letter," the detective said finally. "He told us that Søren Rasmussen wasn't one of his clients, but he did mention that fishing trip. It was actually five years ago, not two. Apparently Mr. Rasmussen made quite an impression on him. Seemed to know the best spots to fish, and he kept the two lawyers entertained with wild Viking stories. Mr. Karovsky said Rasmussen was quite a character, but he hasn't seen him since. He was surprised to hear that his name was on some kind of letter. And we still don't know why Mr. Rasmussen wanted to contact him. There's not much to go on from that letter."

"When exactly did Søren die?" asked Margit, prevailing on the detective's grudgingly accommodating mood. The newspaper report of the murder had been extremely sketchy. Most of the story was given over to journalistic hysterics about the increasing violence in the city, now spreading even to the staid streets of Ballard.

"Sometime early Sunday morning, we think. Can't pinpoint it any closer than that. Why?"

"Just wondering," said Margit. "He was my friend, you know," she added with a genuine quaver in her voice. At that moment Margit decided not to tell the police about the envelope from Søren containing the runes and sketches. She knew this was withholding evidence that might help the case, but something made her keep back the information. She didn't like the detective's tone of voice. He seemed to think that she actually had something to do with both the murder and the break-in.

According to her answering machine, the message from Søren had been recorded at 8:23 on Friday night. This fact she *had* reported to the police.

What puzzled her now was what had happened between the time Søren wrote the unrevealing letter to the lawyer and the time he mailed her the envelope. Something had made him send her a clue to his problem. Something had changed his mind.

5

Margit turned left on NW 58th Street and slowed down as she neared the middle of the block. Then she pulled over to the curb and turned off the engine. She was parked across the street from Søren's house. It was Thursday afternoon, four days after the murder, and the crime scene was still cordoned off with official yellow police tape, flapping in the wind. One piece had come loose and was now waving merrily from the top of the plum tree at the corner of the lot. Margit could see a sign posted on the front door, warning off trespassers and ghoulish spectators. But there was nobody around.

Margit was surprised at her own morbid curiosity. She was actually on her way over to the Nordic Heritage Museum for a 1:30 appointment, but suddenly she found herself turning onto Søren's street, and now here she was, staring at his empty house.

It was a bright sunny day for a change, and warm enough to get by with a lightweight jacket over a long-sleeved shirt. Margit was also wearing her oldest pair of jeans. The worn denim was velvet-soft against her scratched legs, and the pants were comfortably loose, since she'd lost five pounds and a couple of inches around her hips—thanks to her recent exercise regime. She was sitting on a pillow filled with down, cushioning her stitched and bruised behind. The almond latte in the paper cup on the dashboard was making a little circle of steam on the windshield.

Margit rolled down the window and leaned her head out, looking up and down the quiet street. A man in the familiar uniform of the U.S. Postal Service was slowly approaching from the west end of the block. Margit was out of her car in a flash, and by the time the mailman reached Søren's house she was standing in front of the garish yellow tape, eagerly gawking at the scene.

"Wow, this must be where it happened," said Margit, turning to give the mailman a wide-eyed stare. "I read about the murder in the paper."

"Yeah. I did too," said the man, shifting the heavy mailbag to his other shoulder and hitching up his pants as he stopped to look at the vacant, dilapidated house surrounded by tall grass and weeds. He didn't mind taking a little break for a friendly chat. It was so rare to find anybody to talk to on his daily rounds delivering the mail.

"Wonder who did it," said Margit. "Who would want to break into a dump like this and kill an old man? He sure didn't bother to keep up the place, did he? Must have made his neighbors mad to have this eyesore on the block. Guess he was a real hermit.

"Bet he didn't get much mail, either," she added, looking at the man out of the corner of her eye.

"Naw, mostly junk mail and magazines, but sometimes he'd get a letter from overseas. I always noticed the stamp— from Norway or Denmark, I think."

And then he leaned so close to Margit that she could see the enlarged pores of his ruddy skin and smell the onion on his breath. She forced herself not to step back. The mailman lowered his voice to a conspiratorial whisper: "I called the police after I read about the murder, you know. Thought they'd want to hear about anything unusual." He nodded his head and gave Margit a smug look.

"Really?" said Margit. "Did you notice something odd?"

"Well, sort of. When I came by last Saturday, I went up to the old man's house to deliver his monthly fishing magazines and when I opened the mailbox, I found a letter inside, waiting to be mailed. It had a stamp on it and everything. He hardly ever left letters for me to pick up. Maybe two or three times in the ten years I've been doing this route. So it stuck in my mind. Then I read the news in the paper, so I called up the police. They asked me a couple of questions, but they kind of lost interest when I said I couldn't remember who the letter was for. We're not supposed to do that, you know. We're not supposed to *read* the mail we pick up, not even the addresses," he said rather huffily.

"No, of course not," Margit reassured him. "So you always come by about this time of day?"

"Uh-huh," said the mailman, "but last Saturday I was a little late, don't think I got here until after two. I was out with the fellas the night before, so my head was kind of woozy and I was dragging my feet that day." And he gave Margit a wink, running the tip of his tongue along his lower lip. He was still standing too close.

Margit histrionically raised her left arm to her face and stared at her wristwatch. Then she uttered a little shriek and spun on her heel. "I'm late," she yelled over her shoulder as she ran across the street, pulling the car keys out of her jacket pocket. She jumped into the driver's seat, wincing as she sank onto the pillow. Then she slammed the car door and locked it before she turned on the engine.

At that moment her mother's admonishing voice from thirty years ago suddenly filled her ears, "Now Margit, you know *wery vell* that *ve* do not talk to strangers." Margit laughed, hearing in her mind her mother's unmistakable Danish accent—the way she swallowed her "r"s and confused her "v"s and "w"s.

Margit picked up her latte from the dashboard, took a sip, and stomped on the gas pedal. The Mazda shuddered convulsively, lurched forward, and then roared off down the street. Margit had an appointment to keep, and if she didn't step on it, she really was going to be late.

But at least she had found out one important piece of information. Sometime between 8:23 p.m. on Friday, when Søren left the message on Margit's answering machine, and two o'clock on Saturday afternoon, he had changed his mind about keeping his secret to himself. Margit was positive that the letter in Søren's mailbox had been addressed to her.

⌘

Margit parked her car on the wide, tree-lined street in front of the Nordic Heritage Museum. She picked up a folder lying on the seat next to her and tucked her canvas bag under her left arm as she got out of the car. The old brick building of the museum had once been an elementary school, and it reminded Margit of her own grade school back in St. Paul.

She walked up the narrow cement stairs built into the hillside, thinking about those stuffy classrooms, always overheated and smelling of chalk, poster paint, and bologna sandwiches. She remembered squirming restlessly on the slippery chair, fiddling with her pencils, and staring blankly out the window. She was often bored in class because she was such a fast reader that she would finish the assignments long before her classmates were done.

On Margit's first day of school, the teacher had arbitrarily decided to call her "Marge," apparently convinced that all the kids with foreign names would be happier with good old American nicknames. Margit felt her hackles rise every time the teacher uttered that ridiculous name, but she was not alone. Jorge, the boy sitting in front of her, was always addressed as George. And the teacher laughed outright when five-year-old Margit said that her mother's last name was not the same as her father's. "Impossible," the teacher claimed, and that was that. A child's word was no match for the authority of an adult.

Margit turned left and walked past the heavy doors that used to be the entrance to the museum before the recent remodeling. She turned the corner and entered the building on the basement level, stopping at the reception desk in the narrow hall.

Three elderly women were having a cozy chat as they stuffed envelopes for some kind of mailing campaign. The woman with the pink plastic glasses looked up as Margit approached and gave her a welcoming smile. "May I help you, dear?" she asked.

"Yes," said Margit, "I have an appointment with Barbro Ólafsdóttir."

"Oh . . . all right," said the woman, looking a little flustered. "Well, you'll find her in the library upstairs. The elevator's right behind you."

"Thanks," said Margit, and she stepped into the waiting elevator, smiling to herself as the doors slid shut.

Barbro made a lot of people uncomfortable. Margit had met her for the first time back in 1977 at a big international conference for Scandinavian scholars in Minneapolis.

Margit was a graduate student at the university then, finishing up her Masters thesis on the works of the Norwegian writer Amalie Skram. She had attended the conference with mixed feelings, since she was beginning to have serious doubts about her own academic future. All of the latest teaching positions in her field had been filled by so-called "native speakers," imported Scandinavians whose linguistic birthright gave them preference in the U.S. job market over their American counterparts. The universities wanted to hire "real" Danes and Norwegians and Swedes, even though their other credentials were often barely adequate. Margit's mother was Danish and her father was a Swede from Uppsala, but she had been born and raised in St. Paul. Her acquired fluency in the Scandinavian languages did not give her the status of a native speaker.

Margit was trying hard not to panic as she watched her colleagues, most of them with completed Ph.D. dissertations in hand, aced out of jobs by less-qualified foreigners. Her friends were vanishing into the general work force, unable to turn their ten years of higher education into the academic careers they had envisioned. Margit realized that she might have to start thinking about other possibilities herself.

At that time Barbro Ólafsdóttir was an assistant professor

at an obscure college in the East, and she already had a reputation for iconoclastic theories and eccentric behavior, although few people attending the conference had actually met her. She taught Chaucer and Old English, but her specialty was runes.

Margit went to hear Barbro deliver a lecture on a newly discovered runic inscription found on a stone near Bergen. Professor Ólafsdóttir appeared on stage solemnly reciting the opening lines of an Icelandic saga, dressed in a roughly woven hemp tunic and a scanty knee-length cord skirt made from strings fastened at both the top and bottom. Around her waist she wore a bronze belt-plate, which resembled a small shield with a spike in the middle. But even more striking than her unexpected attire was Barbro's obvious lack of any Scandinavian bloodlines. Barbro was Chicana.

The gray-suited professors in the audience gasped. The graduate students cheered. And Barbro's lecture turned out to be just as controversial as her appearance.

Margit found out later that Barbro's real name was Bernice Ramirez, that she grew up in Tucson, and that she had her first dream about Iceland when she was six years old. In school she read all the books she could find about the ancient North. She demanded a copy of Snorri Sturluson's *Heimskringla* for her tenth birthday, and by the time Bernice started college she was an expert on the sagas. She studied Latin, Greek, and Old English. She was fluent in Spanish, Italian, Swedish, and modern Icelandic. But her real obsession was always Old Norse.

When Bernice entered graduate school, she began submitting articles to scholarly journals under the pen name of Barbro Ólafsdóttir because she soon realized that this was the only way her work would be taken seriously. She was all too aware that the majority of arch-conservatives in her chosen field would prefer to exclude her from the club because she lacked the proper ancestry. It was an even bigger disadvantage than her gender. Their tactics were covert and insidious—mavericks were not easily tolerated. So Bernice decided that she needed a Scandinavian cover to gain acceptance, and she chose a name that was half Swedish and half Icelandic, aiming for the highest quotient of respectability. By the time people figured out who was behind the pen name, her work had won too much acclaim to be ignored.

After a few years, Bernice went ahead and made the name official, and she had been Barbro Ólafsdóttir ever since. But her refusal to adapt to the conventional academic modes of behavior eventually got her into trouble, and in 1978 she was denied tenure because of some minor impropriety. The good old boys could barely hide their glee. Barbro dropped out of academia and disappeared from the conference circuit—no one was quite sure what had happened to her.

Then, in 1982, the ground-breaking book *Meditations of a Renegade Runologist* by Barbro Ólafsdóttir was published by a prestigious London house to rave reviews, even in the *New York Times*. Suddenly Barbro was in demand. The universities fell all over themselves with offers of full professorships, but she turned them all down. She actually enjoyed her job as director of the small museum library in Seattle, and she preferred her freedom as an independent scholar to the rigid restraints of any university.

Margit was not the first to make the pilgrimage to the Nordic Heritage Museum to consult the world-famous expert on runes.

She knocked gently on the library door, then pushed it

open and stepped inside. It was a long, narrow room, but every inch of wall space was covered with crowded bookshelves, clear up to the ceiling, fourteen feet above. A ladder on wheels rested against the shelves to the right of the door. Two heavy oak tables with chairs upholstered in dark red leather stood in the center of the room, and four brass desk lamps with green shades cast bright yellow patches of light on the tabletops. Sunlight slanted in through a tall window at the far end of the room. The library was empty except for Barbro, who sat hunched over her desk near the window, reading a manuscript and making notes in the margins. The screen saver on her computer showed an animated version of the Viking raid on Lindisfarne in 793.

"Working on a new book?" asked Margit as she walked past the tables toward Barbro's desk.

"Oh," exclaimed Barbro, giving a start. When she was writing she blocked out everything else; she hadn't even heard the loud creak of the door as it opened. "Margit! How are you?" Barbro leaned back, took off her reading glasses, and grinned as she ran her hand through the soft curls of her short black hair. She was wearing a burgundy sweater, jeans, and a pair of old cowboy boots. The large gold disks of her earrings were replicas of 6th-century *bracteates* with a runic inscription encircling the profile of a big-nosed man. Barbro's full lips were painted bright red.

"I'm starting to feel my age," replied Margit as she gingerly lowered herself onto the hard wooden chair across from Barbro. "And I'm not sure I like it."

"I know what you mean, and I'm eight years older than you. If it's any comfort, the average life expectancy in the 10th century was thirty-five. With any luck, you've still got a good three decades ahead of you. Keep that in mind."

Margit laughed and put the folder she was carrying on top of the desk. She hadn't seen Barbro in a couple of years, but she had read a review of her latest book in the *Seattle Times*, and Barbro was obviously still shaking up the established academic circles with her ideas. The mere fact that her books were read with interest by the general public was antithetical to the tradition of equating obscurity and obtuseness with scholarly brilliance. The reviewer, who for once actually seemed to have some knowledge of the subject, had called Barbro's recent book a masterful achievement.

"How's Hrafnir?" asked Margit, realizing suddenly that Barbro's son must be almost twenty-five by now.

"Great," said Barbro. "He's teaching history to first graders and loves it." Hrafnir had never shared his mother's fascination with the Nordic countries, in spite of numerous trips to Iceland and Sweden when he was a kid. Instead, he had returned to his Hispanic roots, and after finishing college he had moved to Yakima to work in a Chicano community center. Hrafnir was just as much an anomaly as Barbro, since he had inherited the towering height and dazzling white hair of his Icelandic father, Thorsteinn Halldórsson, a noted vulcanologist. On first meeting Hrafnir, few people expected him to speak Spanish, let alone know anything about Chicano history and culture.

"So, you've got some puzzle for me?" said Barbro, her eyes sparkling. She loved the thrill of untangling runic inscriptions, and it was so rare to come upon anything that had not been analyzed a million times before. She was always hoping to make a new discovery.

"I think so," said Margit. "I'm not really sure what it is." She pulled the photocopy with the runes out of the folder and handed it to Barbro.

"Too bad it's so blurry," said Barbro, putting on her reading glasses and squinting at the page. She ran the forefinger of her right hand slowly along each line several times, and for a good five minutes she didn't say a word.

"Huh," she muttered finally, and sighed heavily. She raised her eyes from the paper and peered at Margit over the top of her glasses.

"Well," said Barbro, "the last line could be authentic, but the rest is all wrong. Must have been written by someone with only a rudimentary knowledge of runes. Clearly a fake. Where did you get this, anyway?"

"I can't tell you that," replied Margit, trying hard to stifle her impatience, knowing that Barbro would not like to be hurried. "What do you mean by 'a fake'?"

"Just look at the *futhark* on the second line," said Barbro. "It's all jumbled up."

Margit dutifully glanced down at the page, but her look of sheer incomprehension evoked a loud laugh from the expert.

"Forgotten even the basics, I see," chided Barbro, shaking her head. "Your professor in Old Norse would not be pleased."

Then her expression turned serious and she settled in to explain. "The 24-letter runic alphabet is called the *futhark*, named for the values of the first six letters, or runes. It's divided into three groups of eight runes each, known as *ættir*, or families. We have several examples of the entire *futhark* inscribed on stone and pieces of metal, and the order is always consistent. But your runes are all mixed up. The *ættir* are written in reverse order, which is interesting because runic inscriptions can be bidirectional—although I don't think I've ever seen the *futhark* represented this way. But the runes within each family are all out of place. It's a real mishmash. It has to be a fake."

"What about the rest?" asked Margit, dismayed at Barbro's conclusion, which seemed to cancel out any hope of understanding why Søren had sent her the runes.

"The first line is a bastardization of a famous inscription. It says, 'WigoR is my name, the knower of dangerous things.' There are two misspelled words, obviously miscopied, and the name has been changed from 'Hariuha' to 'WigoR,' which is a most unlikely name, especially for the period."

"And the last line?" asked Margit, now resigned to hearing discouraging news.

"The last line is more interesting," said Barbro thoughtfully, tapping her forefinger on the runes in question. She took off her reading glasses and straightened up as she looked across the desk at Margit.

"It says, 'I, runemaker, offer this horn.'"

6

Friday night was Poetry Slam night at the Cedar Café. Bob was setting up the microphone and speakers on a small platform against the far wall as Margit pulled open the door and came in. The place was deserted, but in another hour it would be packed with earnest-looking poets huddled around the tables, muttering to themselves as they secretly scanned their lines scribbled on scraps of paper. Most of the participants were in their early twenties, although a gray-bearded man wearing beads and a tight tie-dyed shirt occasionally took to the stage, purporting to be a latter-day Ginsberg. No liquor was served in the café, but the number of espressos and lattes consumed during the evening inevitably raised the audience energy level right through the roof. The sloppy intoxication of alcohol was no match for the jittery high of caffeine.

"Hey Bob," said Margit with a wave of her hand, "is Renny here?"

"She'll be back in twenty minutes or so. Went over to Ernst to buy some supplies and another 'No Smoking' sign. Some kids tore up the old one last Friday, and Renny spent the whole night telling people to put out their cigarettes. You know what a fanatic she is. And this is supposed to be a smoke-free place, after all. But there's always a couple of wise guys in the crowd."

"Can I get a salad while I'm waiting for her?" asked Margit, sitting down at a table in a corner of the room, as far away from the stage as possible. She didn't want to get stuck in the middle of the swarm of people that would soon take over the café.

"Sure," said Bob, as he made a final adjustment to the mike and hopped down from the platform. "The Cedar Special?"

"Great," said Margit. "Oil and vinegar on the side. No onions. And mineral water with a slice of lemon."

Bob nodded and headed for the kitchen. The café was always empty right before the Poetry Slam. It was apparently considered uncool to show up too far in advance. People would start sauntering in at 7:45, and by 8:15 Bob would have to turn would-be slammers away. He was amazed at how popular the weekly event had become. Bob had always had a soft spot for poetry, and in his hippie days he had even written some terribly contrived verse himself, before he discovered that cooking was his true art. But he was still skeptical when Renny suggested that the café's Friday-night open mike for folk singers (which he had to admit was poorly attended in recent years) should be scrapped in favor of competitive poetry.

But Renny had been right, and the café had attracted a steady clientele of young writers ever since, even during the rest of the week. Poetry was apparently good for business.

Margit was always amused by the wildly divergent waves of customers descending upon the Cedar, depending on the time of day. From six to eight in the morning, squadrons of shiny new BMWs, Hondas, and four-wheelers would screech to a stop outside the café, disgorging frantic commuters in need of a caffeine fix on their way to work. From nine till noon the young mothers of the neighborhood would stop in for coffee and a chat, their babies gurgling on their laps, a fleet of strollers parked just inside the door. The local business crowd would show up for lunch, and then the café would settle into the quiet afternoon hours, frequented by artists and writers with a more leisurely schedule than other West Seattle residents. Only dinnertime brought a diverse mix of customers, attracted by the café's well-deserved reputation for serving hearty meals made from the freshest ingredients. Bob put all his creativity into his cooking.

Margit leaned back in her chair and closed her eyes for a moment, savoring the temporary silence and solitude. She was tired.

It was hard to believe that it was only five days ago that she had so reluctantly said goodbye to Joe at the Albuquerque airport after a week of exquisite sexual pleasure. She could still feel the heat of his strong sculptor's hands moving over her body as they embraced near the departure gate, oblivious to everyone else in the crowded waiting area. She felt his left hand pressed against the small of her back. His other hand stroked her breasts, making her nipples jump against the fabric of her bra. He moved his hand to her face, and she felt the hard pads of his fingers gently caressing her cheek, smoothing her eyebrow, and running along the rim of her ear. She shivered as he cupped the back of her head, pressing her face toward his. And she sighed at the touch of his lips on her mouth, his tongue flicking fire into her body, making her pulse roar and her mind melt.

"Looks like rain," said Bob, the sudden boom of his voice nearly toppling Margit out of her chair. "You feeling OK?" he added. "You look a little flushed. Not coming down with the flu, are you?"

"I'm fine," replied Margit, blinking rapidly and tucking a loose strand of hair behind her right ear. She felt just like a teenager caught making out with her boyfriend in the back seat of his car. She reached for the mineral water that Bob had set on the table and drank half the glass in one long swallow. The shock of the icy liquid flashed all the way to her toes, and it instantly cleared her head.

"Just feeling a little worn out, is all," said Margit. "It's been a hard week." She glanced appreciatively at the enormous salad and the basket of homemade bread that Bob had placed in front of her. She was suddenly ravenous.

"I can dig that," said Bob, reverting to the slang of his youth, as he often did when he was feeling a little awkward. "Renny told me about you finding that old guy murdered. Shitty thing to happen. Too much violence these days. Way too much violence." Bob shook his head in disgust. "More random acts of kindness are what we need," he continued. "Seen that bumper sticker? 'Commit a random act of kindness,' it says. I like that." And then Bob patted Margit's shoulder clumsily and ambled off toward the espresso bar to take an order from a young man who had just come in and wanted a double tall skinny with vanilla.

Margit unfolded the paper napkin and slipped it onto her lap. She poured a few drops of olive oil and a dash of vinegar over her salad—she was trying to wean herself from using salad dressing altogether. Too many calories. Then she picked up her fork, letting it hover over the mound of red-leaf lettuce, fresh spinach, alfalfa sprouts, carrot strips, papery-thin radishes, and gleaming chunks of avocado. She pushed the olives and three slices of cucumber to the side, conceding that her stomach just couldn't handle certain foods anymore, and then jabbed her fork into a juicy wedge of tomato.

It really *had* been a hard week, thought Margit wearily as she ate her dinner. Too much commotion and upheaval for her normally quiet life. And on top of everything else, her boss had been heaping work on her all week long. When Margit delivered the Thor Cheese job at nine that morning, Liisa had immediately handed her a thick stack of Swedish horticultural articles and told her that half of them were due by six. "They're paying rush rate," Liisa hurried to add when she noticed Margit's look of dismay.

So Margit had spent the rest of the day at the agency, pounding out the translation at lightning speed. She learned all about bottle palms, Chinese evergreens, peace lilies, philodendrons, azaleas, and the Madagascar jasmine, a white flower with an overwhelming scent frequently used in bridal wreaths. She took a half-hour break to zoom over to her doctor's office and get her stitches removed, and then she was back translating long passages on plant nutrients, root balls, and potting soil. By the time she finished, just a couple of minutes before six, she could fully sympathize with the reaction of the weeping fig, which was prone to drop its leaves at the slightest jostling.

Margit walked out of the agency fifteen minutes later, limp with released tension, wondering whether anyone ever fully appreciated what was actually demanded of a translator. It was not enough to be fluent in two or more languages. It was not enough to be an excellent writer with a solid knowledge of syntax and grammar. A translator also had to be able to comprehend and then regurgitate the specialized vocabulary unique to every field. One day it was vitamin supplements, medical ethics, and clinical trials. Then it was the annual report of an airline, a sociological treatise on single-parent families, or an article on a big scandal in the steel industry. Every field had its own jargon that had to be accurately transposed into the equivalent vocabulary of the target language.

Margit had become an expert on many topics that she would never have tackled on her own. She knew more about paper mills than many executives in the business, and she was intimately familiar with the complicated construction (and terrifying weaknesses) of nuclear power plants, simply because of all the documents she had translated on the subject. After fifteen years as a professional translator, Margit no longer hesitated to take on topics that she knew nothing about. She was an old hand at finding the right reference books, or locating an expert in the field to consult if all other resources failed her.

There was something different every day—Margit certainly couldn't complain about being bored by her work. But the avalanche of constantly changing subjects sometimes stretched her poor brain to the limit. At the end of the day she would often curl up in bed with a thick 19th-century novel (Flaubert or Dostoyevsky, George Eliot or Amalie Skram), welcoming the slow pace and steady unfolding of the story.

If her mind refused to handle one more word in *any* language, she would do four loads of laundry and set up the ironing board in the bedroom. Then she'd put on the Temptations or the latest Little Feat album, crank up the volume, and get to work. She ironed absolutely everything: t-shirts, sweaters, blue jeans, sheets, even her underwear. It usually took her hours to finish, but it was soothing and satisfying work that didn't require her to think. She always felt refreshed after one of her ironing binges.

Margit was just finishing her salad when Renny rushed into the café.

"Hi kiddo! How're you doing?" said Renny with a big smile, plunking herself down on the chair across from Margit. She dropped her packages onto the floor and pulled a piece of bread out of the basket on the table.

"Pretty good," said Margit, realizing how quickly a little food could revive her spirits. And Renny always cheered her up too. She was so full of energy and good humor that it was impossible to be glum in her presence. Today she was wearing her hair in dozens of tiny braids with red and silver beads fastened to the ends. The beads clacked softly whenever Renny moved her head.

"Ready for the poetry crowd?" asked Margit.

"Oh sure," said Renny with a laugh. "I actually enjoy listening to the kids, you know. They're so fierce about their work, and it's good to see the younger generation display some passion for a change. A lot of them are pretty good, too. And at least we're keeping them off the streets for one night a week. Who knows—we may be launching the next Beat Generation right here at the Cedar Café." Renny grabbed a second piece of bread, folded it into quarters, and stuffed it into her mouth. She loved bread and swore that she could subsist on a diet of nothing but carbohydrates, if only she weren't so addicted to meat. The smell of a lean New York steak sizzling on the grill was ecstasy for her. She respected Margit's decision to give up meat, but she could never be a vegetarian herself.

"So what did the rune expert say?" asked Renny, leaning eagerly over the table. "Any more clues to Søren's murder?"

"I'm not really sure," said Margit, and then she told Renny about her meeting with Barbro Ólafsdóttir the day before.

"Wow," said Renny when she heard about the translation of the last line of runes. "'I, runemaker, offer this horn,'" she repeated, enunciating each word carefully, savoring the drama of the sentence. "Did you tell Barbro about the pictures from the Golden Horns?"

"Yes," said Margit. "I wasn't going to at first, but the minute Barbro read that last line of runes, she started wondering about a connection with the horns. So I finally told her the whole story, and I'm glad I did. It turned out that she knew all the details about the discovery and disappearance of the horns, and it's an amazing tale. Everything went wrong right from the start."

"What do you mean?"

"Just listen to this," said Margit. "When Kirsten Svendsdatter literally stumbled on the first Golden Horn in a South Jutland field in 1639, she did the right thing and turned it over to the king. At that time, the law of the land proclaimed that any treasures unearthed in Denmark were royal property. But the king forgot to give her any compensation for her incredible discovery, so she went to the trouble of petitioning, ever so humbly, for a reward. And believe me, that girl needed the money. She was an orphan, eking out a living by selling bits of lace. So guess what the king's representative gave the poor girl for finding the fabulous ancient treasure?"

"What?" asked Renny, all ears.

"A skirt! One lousy skirt," said Margit, filled with outrage on the girl's behalf, more than three centuries after the fact.

"Geez," said Renny, "that's disgusting."

"It gets worse," Margit went on. "King Christian IV ordered the horn to be reshaped into a goblet, but luckily one of his advisors dissuaded him. Then he decided to give the treasure to the crown prince, who plugged up the end with a piece of gold so it could be used as a drinking horn at royal banquets."

"I can just picture the scene," said Renny. "A bunch of drunken dukes tossing around the priceless Golden Horn."

"Uh-huh," said Margit, grimacing at the thought. "About fifty years later, somebody finally came to his senses and put the horn in the Royal Art Chamber for safekeeping. Then, in 1734, a farmer named Erich Lassen found a second Golden Horn in practically the same spot, and he ran home all excited, shouting for a bottle of aquavit to celebrate. The farmer ended up getting a better deal than the lace-maker. The local nobleman gave him a reward of 200 *Rigsdaler*, but Erich Lassen didn't get to enjoy his good fortune. He died three weeks after receiving the money, and his mean-spirited neighbors made sure that this decent man was remembered forever as a wretched drunk, simply because he had innocently called for a toast to celebrate his good luck."

"What slimes," declared Renny. "Sounds like the Golden Horns didn't bring anybody good luck."

"No," Margit agreed, "they didn't."

"So what about the thief?" asked Renny. "What was the guy's name ... Niels Hildenrick?"

"Heidenreich," said Margit. "A real loser. Came from a troubled family in Jutland and was already mixed up in petty theft as a kid. In 1788 he was arrested in Copenhagen for printing counterfeit bills, and he was ordered to relinquish both his possessions and his life. But King Christian VI commuted his sentence to life imprisonment, and nine years later Heidenreich was back out on the streets. The king even granted him the right to run a small watch-repair and goldsmith shop on Larsbjørnstræde, in the heart of the city."

"So the king was an unwitting accomplice to the theft of his own treasures," said Renny with some satisfaction.

"Yes," replied Margit. "Ironic, isn't it? Anyway, at that time the Golden Horns were on display in the Antiquities Room of the Royal Art Chamber, which was housed in a gallery of the Royal Library. One day a bad storm caused such severe water damage to the building that the connecting door between the library and the art chamber had to be temporarily opened — it was normally locked and covered with a tapestry. Well, our friend Niels Heidenreich just happened to pay a visit to the library that day, and he noticed that it was possible to gain access to the art chamber through the library. Since he was once again in dire straits, with a family to support and creditors at his heels, Niels decided to steal the Golden Horns. He made himself a duplicate key to the outer door of the library, and on the night of May 4, 1802, he committed the theft. Amazingly enough, he was able to open all the interior locks in the building with his own house key."

"Great security system," said Renny with a laugh. "So he took the horns home and melted them down. How did he get caught?"

"A fellow goldsmith got suspicious because Niels suddenly seemed to have plenty of gold on hand for his work, so he reported Niels to the police. But that was almost a whole year after the horns were stolen. The investigation was a complete joke. At first the police tried to suppress the news of the theft; then they finally had to admit that they didn't have a single clue."

"Same old story," said Renny.

"I know. And all that time, Niels Heidenreich sat right there in the middle of Copenhagen, melting down the irreplaceable treasures in his kitchen. He shaped the gold into shoe buckles, necklaces, and replicas of coins, called 'pagodas.'"

"You mean 'pagoda,' like one of those temples?" asked Renny, looking puzzled.

"Same word, different meaning," Margit told her. "They were small, crudely minted coins from India that were easy to counterfeit and highly marketable at the time. Niels sold off almost 800 of them, and made enough money to buy himself a new house. I guess that's what finally made the other goldsmith suspicious."

"Greed and jealousy—the downfall of every criminal," pronounced Renny. "So that was the end of the Golden Horns?"

"Yes. The authorities rounded up a lot of the items that Niels had made from the ancient gold, but they couldn't account for all of them. And the only accurate replicas of the horns mysteriously disappeared in Germany. In the mid-1800s, King Frederik VII had a goldsmith make reconstructions of the horns, and they're still on display in the National Museum today. But everybody knows that they're flawed and based on contradictory sketches."

"The gifts of the past were unappreciated and mistreated, so they were taken back—lost to future generations for good," mused Renny, as she took the last piece of bread out of the basket on the table.

"That's exactly what Oehlenschlæger said in his famous poem," exclaimed Margit. "And by a strange twist of fate, he lived only a few blocks away from Niels Heidenreich's goldsmith shop. So at the very moment that the thief was melting down the horns, the poet was writing his inspired verse."

"Talk about ironic," said Renny gleefully.

At that moment Bob came up to their table and handed Margit the cordless phone he was carrying.

"Call for you," he said, and then he turned to Renny. "Place is starting to fill up. Think you could give me a hand?"

"Oh God, yes," said Renny, picking up her packages from the floor and scrambling to her feet. "Sorry. I got so wrapped up in what Margit was telling me that I forgot all about the time." And Renny rushed off, yelling "Great story" over her shoulder to Margit as she left.

Margit pressed the talk button on the phone and said, "Hello?"

"Miss Andersson? Detective Tristano here. Your boss told us we might find you at this number."

Oh great, thought Margit. Why do the police have to keep bothering Liisa?

"There's been an attempted burglary at your place," continued the detective.

"What!" shouted Margit, attracting the attention of the people at a nearby table. "What are you talking about?"

"One of your neighbors—a Mr. Nettlebury—reported hearing a loud noise, and when he looked out the window he saw a man running full-speed out of your house. He said the man jumped into a dark blue Volvo and headed south."

"I can't believe this," moaned Margit with a frown, impatiently brushing her hair back from her face. "What the hell is going on, anyway?"

"We were hoping that *you* might be able to answer that question, Miss Andersson," said Detective Tristano softly.

Margit didn't like the implication, but she had no idea how to counter it. This guy really got on her nerves.

"We sent an officer over to investigate," the detective continued, "and your neighbor told him that the burglar seemed to be bleeding from his face and arms. Do you have a watchdog, Miss Andersson?"

"No, I don't," said Margit faintly. "I have a cat."

7

At 10:30 on Saturday morning, Margit was on her way over to Queen Anne to meet with Detective Tristano to "have a little chat," as he put it. She drove by Renny's house to see whether she could persuade her friend to come along, realizing that she was feeling a little vulnerable. It would boost her confidence to have an ally at the meeting. But Renny had put the "Artist At Work—Do Not Disturb" sign on her door, which meant that for the next twelve hours or so she would be incommunicado. When she was painting she didn't even answer the phone. Margit sighed and turned the Mazda around, heading back toward SW Admiral.

OK, she told herself, you're a grown woman, you can handle this yourself. You haven't done anything wrong, so why should you let this guy scare you? Just don't let him tick you off, Margit. Keep cool.

She pulled into the crowded Starbucks lot and ordered a triple grande to go. She needed a good jolt of caffeine to get her through this interview with the police.

Then Margit headed down the hill toward the West Seattle

bridge, casting a fleeting glance at the distant city skyline visible from the viewpoint on her left. She popped a Mary-Chapin Carpenter cassette into the tape deck, fast-forwarded to the tune "He Thinks He'll Keep Her," and automatically sang along, even though her thoughts were on the events of the night before.

⌘

Margit still couldn't believe that someone had actually broken into her house. She knew that crime was on the rise, and she always took the normal precautions, but she had decided long ago that she was not going to live her life consumed by paranoia. A few years back her wallet was stolen when she put it down on a counter in the bank, of all places. And someone had once smashed the right rear window of her car, apparently assuming that the plastic bag of mint leaves on the back seat actually contained dope. But otherwise Margit had been lucky. It made her shiver just thinking about some strange man wandering around in her house and touching her things.

Nothing seemed to be missing, but the guy had opened the file cabinet in her study and pulled out half the files, tossing them on the floor in a heap. He had also rummaged through the big box labeled *"Breve,"* and Margit wondered whether the burglar could actually read the Danish label, or whether he had stumbled onto her correspondence by accident. He had switched on her computer, but she had forgotten to remove her backup disk from the floppy drive, so the opening sequences had stalled halfway through. At that point, Gregor had apparently entered the scene.

My hero, thought Margit with a laugh. She knew that

Gregor was fiercely protective of his territory, and especially his furniture, but she had no idea that he was capable of assault.

When she drove up to her house the night before and jumped out of the car, Gregor had trotted down the pathway to meet her, his eyes defiant and his fur standing on end. He growled loudly, refused to be petted, and then headed straight back to the house, stationing himself squarely in front of the door, which was still slightly ajar. There was blood sprinkled on the pathway and steps. And when Margit poked her head through the front door, she could see a trail of red dots on the carpet leading through the living room toward the study.

"Glad you're home," shouted Margit's next-door neighbor, Mr. Nettlebury, who was sitting on his front porch with a baseball bat on his lap, keeping a close eye on her place. He was all bundled up in a plaid wool jacket with a scarf around his neck, gloves on his hands, and a Mariners baseball cap on his head. The temperature had dropped to 44 degrees, and it was cold to be sitting outdoors in one spot. "I'm gonna be late for work, but I promised the police I'd stay till you got back," he told her.

Mr. Nettlebury was seventy-one, a widower, and a retired machinist whom Margit seldom saw because he slept during most of the day. He had a job working the night shift at the local MiniMart. Like so many senior citizens, Mr. Nettlebury had discovered that his pension and social security checks were not enough to cover his monthly expenses. "So much for enjoying my Golden Years," he once told Margit with a wry smile. But he considered himself lucky because at least he could still make his house payments, unlike many of his peers.

"That cat of yours is sure one mean dude," said Mr.

Nettlebury. He'd been picking up expressions from the eighteen-year-olds he worked with at the store. "I heard a scream and a bunch of yowling and then I saw that guy come flying out your front door with blood all over his arms and face. Lucky he was wearing gloves or his hands would have been bleeding too. I don't mind telling you that it scared me silly, so I called the police. I couldn't imagine what was going on over there. I never thought your cat could tear someone up like that."

"I know," said Margit. "It's a shock to me too. Poor Gregor must have felt really threatened to do something like that. But thanks for keeping an eye on my place. I really appreciate it. Makes me feel a lot safer with you next door."

"Oh, go on," mumbled Mr. Nettlebury, looking both embarrassed and flattered.

"No, really," insisted Margit. "I mean it." And then she stood on the top step and waved as her neighbor climbed into his old Dodge with the cracked windshield and rusty chrome and headed off to work. Tomorrow she would buy him a five-pound box of his favorite See's chocolates as a thank you.

Margit went into her house with a feeling of nausea and anger and turned on every single light. This couldn't be happening to her—not all in one week. Something was going on that she didn't understand, something ominous and terrifying. And she hated this sense of not being in control. She didn't even like surprise parties, and here she was mixed up in a murder, two burglaries, and some kind of cryptic message from a dead man. She really couldn't take much more of this.

Margit pushed the front door closed and examined the locks. The one in the center of the doorknob was still working, but it was too flimsy to do much good, and the deadbolt was totally shot. She was going to have to barricade her front door shut for the night and call in the locksmith tomorrow. At weekend rates, that wasn't going to be cheap, and she hoped her homeowner's insurance would cover it.

Then Margit went into the kitchen and got out a can of Kitty Stew. "A double portion for you tonight," she told Gregor, smiling at him fondly. "What a watch-cat you are."

And Gregor hunkered down in front of his dish, grumbling and purring contentedly over his food.

⌘

It took Margit a frustrating ten minutes of circling the lower Queen Anne district before she finally found a parking spot. Mary-Chapin was just singing the last lines of "Passionate Kisses" when Margit saw a red Lexus pull out from the curb, and she swiftly nosed her dented Mazda into the empty slot. She couldn't believe it was already so crowded on a Saturday morning. She filled the meter with the requisite eight quarters, getting a mere two hours for her money. It wasn't so long ago that a couple of dimes bought the same amount of time. Things are really getting out of hand these days, Margit thought with a sigh. She wondered how people with big families ever managed to keep up with their expenses.

Margit walked down the street and turned the corner, looking for the Starburst restaurant, where the detective had suggested they meet. He was investigating another case in the area and didn't want to waste time going back to the station. Margit found the Starburst in the middle of the block. It was a little hole-in-the-wall joint with a narrow aisle flanked by a long counter and stools on one side, and vinyl booths on the other. The air was hazy with cigarette smoke. The place looked as if it hadn't changed since the fifties; a lot of the clientele probably hadn't either. Two patrolmen were seated at the counter, and a third walked past her toward the restrooms in the back of the restaurant. The Starburst seemed to be particularly popular with the men in blue, but Margit didn't notice any female officers.

"Miss Andersson?" said a voice from the booth nearest the door.

Margit turned to see a man with black hair and a neatly trimmed mustache sliding out of the seat to stand up and shake her hand. He was tall and athletic-looking, and he was wearing a white shirt, navy-blue blazer, and khaki pants. His plain black tie was held in place by a gold emblem with an insignia that was too small for Margit to read. He was a lot younger than he sounded on the phone. In fact, he looked about twenty-five. Margit wondered how such a preppy young man got to be a homicide detective.

"I'm Detective Tristano," he said. "We met once before, at the murder scene."

"Oh, right," said Margit, suddenly remembering that this was the officer who had made such disparaging remarks about the mess in Søren's house. She hadn't recognized him at first because he had been wearing a uniform that day.

"Would you like some coffee? Or something to eat?" he asked brusquely as they took their seats across from each other.

"A cup of tea would be nice," said Margit, shuddering at the thought of what the coffee would be like in this kind of place. She put her canvas bag down next to her and unbuttoned her jean jacket.

The detective flagged down the waitress and ordered black coffee for himself and "tea for the lady." Then he leaned back, put his right arm along the top of the booth, and stared up at the slowly spinning fan on the ceiling for a moment.

Margit was reminded of a psychology article she once translated which claimed that the more intense a conversation, the farther back a man would sit in his chair, trying to look as relaxed as possible. A woman, on the other hand, would lean closer and closer to the person she was talking to, trying to narrow the distance between them. Margit deliberately leaned back against the peeling orange vinyl of the booth, folded her hands demurely in her lap, and assumed a noncommittal expression.

"So," said the detective, dropping his gaze to give Margit an appraising look. "Still feeling the effects of your fall out the window the other night?"

"Not at all," replied Margit, irritated by the question even though the scratches on her legs were still bothering her a little. "I feel fine." But the officer's youthful face and impeccable attire suddenly made her feel both old and grubby.

The detective nodded, gave her a sharp look, and then said, "Things seem to be getting a little complicated, wouldn't you say so?"

Margit immediately crossed her arms, hunched up her shoulders, and frowned, relinquishing all pretense of a casual appearance. "Well, it hasn't exactly been a normal work week, if that's what you mean," she said crisply, shaking her hair back from her face.

The waitress appeared and set two steaming mugs on the table. Detective Tristano took a sip of his coffee before he continued.

"You and I seem to have gotten off on the wrong foot, Miss Andersson," he said, trying to sound friendly. "How about a truce? We don't have much to go on with this case, and you seem to be involved whether you like it or not. We could use your cooperation."

Margit looked into the detective's brown eyes and relented a little. He reminded her vaguely of a boy in eighth grade whom she had secretly had a crush on. Maybe it was just inexperience that gave him a slightly belligerent edge. "OK," she said, leaning forward. She rested her right elbow on the table and put her chin on her hand. "What do you want to know?"

"We're working on the assumption that there's a link between the attempted burglaries and the murder. On Monday morning you find Mr. Rasmussen's body. On Tuesday someone breaks into your place of employment, and last night a man breaks into your house. Both times the burglar ignores any valuables in the place and goes straight for the file cabinets instead. Somebody is looking for something, and they obviously think that you've got it. Any idea what it might be, Miss Andersson?"

Margit had already realized that the burglars didn't seem to be interested in expensive stereo or computer equipment. They were obviously looking for something specific, and she thought she knew what it was: those two sheets of paper that Søren had sent her. The sketches and runes were apparently worth the risk of breaking-and-entering; they might even have been the cause of Søren's death. But so far she hadn't told the police about their existence, and something was still making her hesitate.

Margit stared at the detective intently and then made up

her mind. "What if I told you that this whole thing has something to do with a couple of 5th-century gold artifacts that disappeared in Denmark in 1802?"

"I'd say that sounds pretty far-fetched," the detective said skeptically, "but I'd like to know why you think so."

Margit reached for her bag and pulled out the sheet of paper with the sketches. "Søren sent me this," she said. And she told the detective about the envelope arriving at her house, about recognizing Søren's handwriting, and about finding two of the same pictures in the book on Danish antiquities. Then she briefly outlined the history of the Golden Horns. But she didn't say a word about the runes.

Detective Tristano leaned forward to pick up the piece of paper and stared at the three figures: the bird pecking at the fish, the three-headed man holding a goat, and the woman with the swirling hair. When Margit finished her story, he folded the paper carefully and stuck it in the pocket of his blazer. Then he leaned back against the vinyl of the booth.

"Withholding evidence is a very serious matter, Miss Andersson. Why didn't you tell us about this before?"

"I didn't think it was important," she said weakly, annoyed with herself for blushing at his stern tone. She picked up her mug and took a sip of the hot tea. It tasted faintly of dish soap.

"Everything related to the case is important," said Detective Tristano. "I want to remind you of your civic obligations here, Miss Andersson. Is there anything else you haven't told us? You've got a clean record so far, except for a few speeding violations and parking tickets. You wouldn't want to get hauled in for obstructing a murder investigation."

"You've been checking up on me?" sputtered Margit, setting down the heavy china mug with a thump.

"Purely routine," said the detective mildly. "Nothing for you to worry about."

"Worry about! All of a sudden I'm a suspect in a murder case, and you tell me there's nothing to worry about? I hope you remember that I was in Santa Fe last Sunday morning, so I couldn't be sticking a knife in the back of some poor old fisherman in Ballard." Margit was leaning over the table and her hands were clenched into fists.

"Take it easy. I didn't say you were a suspect. We check up on everybody when we're working on a homicide. We have to. That's our job. And we're fully aware of your whereabouts last weekend, Miss Andersson. We're not accusing you of killing Søren Rasmussen."

"But you think I'm involved in some way, don't you? You think I had something to do with this whole mess." Margit was so mad that she was practically spitting out her words.

"Calm down, Miss Andersson. There's no reason to get so worked up. You and I are just having a nice little chat about the case. That's all."

Margit stared at the detective's neat black mustache and bland brown eyes. She resented his easy self-confidence, his patronizing tone, and his youthful good looks. Lately she had begun to notice that all the professionals she encountered these days were at least fifteen years younger than she was. Even the president of her bank was only thirty. The world was being run by mere kids, and she couldn't understand how this had happened. Margit certainly didn't feel old—she didn't even think of herself as middle-aged—but sitting across from Detective

Tristano, she suddenly felt the full weight of her years. And she didn't like it.

"At my age," said Margit, sitting up straight and giving the detective a glare, "I don't have to take this kind of shit, even from a cop." And then she grabbed her bag, slid along the bench, and stood up in the aisle. It wasn't easy to make a dignified exit from a booth.

"But Miss Andersson," protested Detective Tristano, looking genuinely startled.

"It's *Ms.* Andersson," hissed Margit. "Not *Miss.* And I've had enough for today." Then she turned on her heel and fled out the door before she had time to regret her impulsive behavior.

It was raining lightly, but Margit didn't notice. She walked briskly down the street and around the corner to her car. She turned the key in the lock, sank into the driver's seat, and yanked the door shut. Then she sat motionless for a few moments, angrily clutching the steering wheel with both hands.

She was glad that she had decided not to mention anything about the runes to Detective Tristano. She knew she was being irrational, but there was something about his dapper clothes and smug voice that jangled her nerves. He wasn't going to get any more "cooperation" from her today.

Margit turned the key in the ignition, noting with annoyance that the windshield was wet. She switched on the intermittent wipers and shoved a cassette into the tape deck as she pulled away from the curb with a screech.

Then she turned up the volume, tilted her head back, and joined Aretha in a ferocious rendition of "Respect."

8

Margit spent the next few hours on Saturday translating
the second batch of Swedish horticultural articles that
Liisa had given her the day before. She had to admit that she was
beginning to feel a little embarrassed by her tantrum at the
Starburst restaurant, but she refused to give in to an internal
voice urging her to call up the detective and apologize.

Let him stew for a few days, she thought. He was the one
who should apologize, anyway. The man needed a serious atti-
tude adjustment. Maybe by the middle of the week she'd change
her mind and hand over the runes. Maybe she wouldn't.

At three o'clock she decided to take a break, and she was
just sitting down to a bowl of potato soup when the telephone
rang.

Margit debated for a few seconds whether to answer it at
all, reminding herself of Joe's philosophy that a ringing phone
was merely an invitation, not a command.

"Don't let it run your life," he always told her. "If you
don't want to talk, just let it ring. Or better yet, pull out the

plug." Which is what he frequently did when he was busy working on a new sculpture, but sometimes he forgot to plug it back in again. And he didn't believe in answering machines.

On one occasion, Margit got so worried when she couldn't reach him for a full ten days that she hopped on the next plane to Albuquerque, rented a car, and drove at breakneck speed to Santa Fe. She pulled up to Joe's studio, expecting to find him delirious with fever, or worse.

But there was Mrs. Herbert McKenzie, the despised Matron, coming down the steps, laughing over her shoulder at a healthy-looking Joe waving from the doorway. Needless to say, Margit was furious, and the incident provoked their first real fight.

After they stopped shouting at each other, Margit suggested they communicate by e-mail instead of relying on the phone. But at that time Joe was still refusing to buy himself a computer, convinced that he would get addicted to Tetris and other computer games and be distracted from his art.

Then Margit came up with a solution that satisfied them both. She bought Joe a fax machine and installed it in his bathroom—the one place where he was sure to see it. Now when she couldn't reach him by phone, she would send him a fax. If he was in the midst of a project and unwilling to be interrupted, Joe had agreed to scribble a quick reply to let her know he was still alive.

Margit's phone rang again. She wasn't as immune to its insistent clamor as Joe and Renny were, and she didn't want to miss an important call. As a freelancer with no guarantee of a steady paycheck, she couldn't afford to lose out on a job just because she didn't feel like answering the phone.

She put a plate on top of her soup to keep it hot and picked up the kitchen extension, fervently hoping that it was not Detective Tristano on the line.

"Yes?"

"This is Mr. Sanders at the Wilcox Funeral Home," said a low, solemn voice in her ear. "I am trying to reach a Mrs. Andersson."

"Speaking," said Margit, deciding not to argue with the "Mrs."

The deep gloom of the man's voice took her back to the summer when she was thirteen years old and staying with her Uncle Hans in Odense. He was a Lutheran minister with an aging congregation, and he frequently got calls from undertakers, who all had that same dismal, commiserating tone of voice. "It's for you," Margit would shout to her uncle after picking up the phone and listening to only a few syllables. "Another *bedemand*."

Her distaste for the carefully modulated tones of those professional consolers had stayed with her ever since.

"Ah, Mrs. Andersson," said Mr. Sanders somberly. "We are so sorry to trouble you at this difficult time, but we are handling the arrangements for the family of the deceased, and we have been asked to give you a message."

"A message from Søren's family?" asked Margit in surprise.

"Yes, that is correct," replied the undertaker, giving equal weight to every word. "Mrs. Karin Fønsgård, the sister of the deceased, would like you to call her at her home in Denmark at your earliest convenience. She wishes to assure you that she will reimburse you for the expense. As far as we can determine, she is available to take your call any day between the hours of nine and eleven a.m., but it is unclear to us whether she means Danish or Seattle time. Her English is, unfortunately, not the best."

I bet her English is a lot better than your Danish, thought Margit with a flash of impatience, noting the way Mr. Sanders had mispronounced Karin's last name. Why did Americans always expect the rest of the world to speak English when most of them made so little effort to learn another language themselves?

"All right," said Margit, keeping her voice polite. "Do you have her phone number?"

"Yes, of course," replied Mr. Sanders, and he slowly read off the eight digits.

"Is Mrs. Fønsgård coming over here for the funeral?" asked Margit after she had copied down the number.

"There will be no funeral," said Mr. Sanders mournfully, obviously dismayed at not being able to provide the full services of the Wilcox Funeral Home (and extract the full remuneration for those services). "The family has decided on cremation and the ashes are to be sent to Denmark for burial in that country, as soon as the police release the body."

"I see." Margit refused to allow the image of Søren's dead form to overtake her consciousness. "Well, thank you for calling, Mr. Sanders."

"Not at all, Mrs. Andersson, we are more than happy to assist you."

And then Margit said goodbye and hung up, glad to be rid of the man's earnest but unwanted sympathy.

She wrote herself a note to call Karin Fønsgård in the morning, between nine and eleven. The times that Søren's sister had given the funeral director had to be Seattle times. Århus was nine hours later, and Margit would have had to stay up past midnight to reach Karin in Denmark during the morning. It seemed most unlikely that Søren's sister would want to inconvenience a complete stranger in that way.

Margit went into her study and stuck the note on the edge of her computer screen so she would see it in the morning. Then she opened the front door to let Gregor in. He was hanging onto the outside doorknob, kicking his back feet against the wood paneling and making a ruckus, as usual. Someday he was going to figure out how to open that door himself, out of sheer frustration.

Then Margit went back to her bowl of soup, wondering what on earth Søren's sister wanted to talk to her about.

⌘

At 6:50 that evening, Margit sat down on the couch and picked up the remote to turn on the TV. Gregor trotted in from the bedroom, jumped up onto her lap, and settled down to watch his favorite program, which lasted all of five minutes. They were both ardent fans of the weekly Lotto show, joining half the people in the state who were sitting tensely in front of the tube, hoping against hope that they would be the next millionaires. At 6:55 the lottery logo flashed on the screen, the familiar music started up, and all the viewers collectively held their breath.

Margit had gotten into the habit of buying a lottery ticket every week, succumbing to Renny's argument that the chance of hitting the jackpot was certainly worth a buck, no matter how astronomical the odds.

"Somebody's gotta win eventually," Renny would say as she handed her dollar and completed lotto slip to the 7-11 clerk. "And it might as well be me."

She always played the same six numbers, positive that some day they were going to be the lucky ones. Margit let the computer choose her numbers at random, always a little embarrassed to find herself buying another ticket and in a hurry to get out of the store.

Gregor purred loudly on Margit's lap, his eyes fixed on the jumping balls on the TV screen. They looked like ordinary Ping-Pong balls skittering around in a waterless fish tank, but each of them was marked with a number. Blasts of air were making them tumble and roll, until six of the balls finally shot through the Plexiglas tubes into position. Margit picked up her ticket to compare the numbers. Not a single match, she realized with a sigh.

And then she gasped and jumped up, dumping Gregor unceremoniously onto the floor.

The sight of those six digits printed on the lottery ticket had suddenly given her an idea. Margit ran down the stairs to her basement library, flicked on the overhead lights, and walked swiftly up and down the aisles, running her right forefinger along the rows of books as she scanned the titles. She bent down to peer at the volumes on the lower shelves, but she couldn't find what she was looking for.

Damn it, she cursed softly to herself. She must have gotten rid of that Old Norse book, after all. She glanced at her wristwatch. It was only 7:15, so there was still plenty of time to make it to the university library.

Margit switched off the lights and ran back upstairs. She grabbed her shoulder bag, picked up the car keys from the hall table, and took her jean jacket out of the closet before she opened the front door. Gregor streaked out of the house and down the pathway a split second before she pulled the door shut and turned the key in the shiny new lock.

Twenty minutes later Margit turned left off of 15th Avenue NE and drove into the cavernous underground parking garage at the university. She whizzed past the attendant's booth, empty at this time of night, and drove down the ramp into the maze of low-ceilinged parking levels. She headed for the east side of the C level, which would get her as close to the library entrance as possible. Cruising up and down the rows, she finally found a slot only a few hundred feet from the stairway door. Nearly every parking place was taken, but there wasn't a soul around.

Margit turned off the engine, cutting off her Van Morrison tape in mid-tune. Fifteen years ago she had parked in this lot four or five times a week, still determined at that time to forge an academic career for herself. Her Masters thesis on Amalie Skram had been published in Norway by a respectable house, and several articles she had written on contemporary Danish authors had already been accepted by literary journals. Margit had also started in on a retranslation of a 19th-century Norwegian novel that had been disgracefully neglected in the English-speaking world. So in 1979, when she entered the doctoral program in Seattle, she was full of enthusiasm, optimism, and false hopes.

After a year, Margit finally realized that academia would never welcome her with open arms. She was too sensible and too outspoken to put up with the backbiting and political conniving that constantly undermined the purported pursuit of knowledge. The tenured faculty in her field preferred to hire meek and dutiful colleagues who would be no threat to their own narrow career ambitions. And they were not interested in having their meager attempts at scholarship upstaged by someone who had already been published as a grad student. Margit decided that Stravinsky's apt appraisal of music critics as "small and rodent-like with padlocked ears" could also apply to some of the professors she knew.

So she gave up her dreams of a university life and found a job with an international import company instead, ultimately relieved at escaping the cloistered campus. She was glad to be out in the real world. Her job gave her a chance to travel, and the lessons she learned about business had proved extremely useful when she eventually decided to become a freelancer.

Margit shook her head. She could hardly remember herself as that idealistic young grad student—it seemed so long ago.

She climbed out of the Mazda with her bag under her arm, pushed down the lock, and shut the door.

At that moment a car suddenly careened around the corner at the far end of the lot and screeched to a stop, the beams of its headlights quivering in the dim light of the parking garage. The car paused—and then roared into gear and headed straight for her, very fast. It was a dark blue Volvo.

For a fraction of a second, Margit stood gaping at the approaching vehicle. Then her reflexes took over and she whirled around and sped toward the green Exit sign, her feet pounding in sync with her thundering heart.

She made it to the heavy exit door, which she wrenched open with her right hand, sending sharp twinges into her shoulder and neck. She raced up the first flight of stairs, her breath coming in tight little gasps. She heard the shriek of skidding tires behind her, the slam of a door, and then the sound of scrambling feet. He was in the stairwell.

Margit reached the first landing and took the next flight of stairs two at a time, commanding her feet to move, move, move. The hairs on the back of her neck stood on end, and she could feel him getting closer.

She made it to the top of the stairs, which opened onto the vast brick expanse of Red Square, a favorite venue for skateboarders during the day, but deserted now. Margit felt the cool night air fill her straining lungs, momentarily stunning her. She groaned and urged herself forward, but it was no use—her feet were like lead and her body refused to go any farther. Furious, she spun around to face her assailant. He wasn't going to take her without a fight.

A swarm of shouting students suddenly burst out of the nearby administration building and flooded around her. They were carrying placards and shaking their fists, glaring up at the lighted windows above them. "Save Ethnic Studies," it said on their signs. The crowd was in an angry mood—the meeting with university officials had obviously not gone well. The students flowed around Margit, half of them moving off across the square, still shouting, while the other half rushed noisily down the steps toward the parking garage.

In a daze, Margit peered down into the stairwell at the figure of a dark-clothed man struggling against the onslaught of shouting students. He was trapped on the last landing, helplessly pinned against the wall. There was nothing he could do but wait for the crush to pass. The light was too dim to see the man's features clearly, but as he turned his face upward, it was impossible to miss the cruel red scratches marring his left cheek.

My God, thought Margit, her eyes widening. It's him. And then she turned on her heel and ran across Red Square, up the wide steps to the library, and in the front entrance.

9

S he is walking naked through a barren landscape. There is nothing beautiful or compelling about this place. It is all cracked earth, glaring heat, and dry lakebeds without a scrap of vegetation—not one single plant to thrust up from the parched ground and wave little tendrils of leaves at the blinding light.

She is walking along a rutted road, kicking up dust, and trudging forward. The horizon is flat and unenticing. She is walking because there is nothing else to do, she has no other options, she can think of no other choice. Her feet fall into place, she puts one foot in front of the other, she swings her arms slightly. She looks ahead and sees only dull gray sky and more cracked brown earth. She has no idea how long she has been walking. She is not hungry, not even thirsty. She has no desires, no needs, her body is making no demands. Her mind is blank. She has been reduced to the simple command to walk: put one foot down, raise the other foot up, take another step. She has no memory and no sense of time. She is a mere shell, a husk, a mechanical toy that has been wound up tight and is slowly unwinding.

Sooner or later she will stop. She will have no more energy to go on, she will lose even the impetus to walk. She will surrender to the landscape, she will sink down on the cracked ground, she will stretch out flat on her back. She will put her arms over her head, she will spread out her legs, she will lie there looking up at the leaden sky. And then she will close her eyes and yield to the hollowness. She will let go of the last urge to move. She will inhale, exhale, and then even that will stop. She will give up entirely, no longer moving, no longer breathing, lying there limp and empty, sinking into the cracks of the ground, swallowed up by the earth.

Margit screamed herself awake and sat bolt upright in bed. Her nightgown was soaking wet, and beads of sweat were trickling down her temples and dripping off her chin. She was shaking violently, and her throat was pinched tight, making her breathing forced and shallow. She snapped on the lamp on the nightstand and wiped her face with the comforter cover.

Not again, Margit moaned softly. Not again. She'd had this dream several times before, and the sense of utter desolation was a thousand times more terrifying than any monstrous images some film director might conjure up. She reached for her water glass and took a long swallow. Then she glanced over at the alarm clock, nodding wearily at the expected configuration of red digits displayed—3:17. She always woke up at exactly the same time when she had this dream. It was eerie, and it gave her the creeps.

Margit threw back the covers and got out of bed. She pulled off her sodden nightgown and tossed it into the clothes hamper. Then she put on her warm terrycloth robe, stuck her bare feet into a pair of moccasins, and trudged out to the kitchen to make herself some chamomile tea. There was no point in trying to go back to sleep for a while. She might as well get up and do something useful.

Gregor had rushed into the bedroom when he heard Margit scream, but now he was hunched over his dish next to the stove, crunching loudly on the dry cat food. When Margit came into the kitchen and switched on the light over the sink, he glanced up and then headed straight for the living room, pointing his nose at the front door and grumbling to be let out. He knew better than to bother Margit when she was asleep, but once she was up, he felt free to make his demands known. And the opportunity for a three a.m. survey of his territory was an unexpected treat.

Margit put the teakettle on the stove and then opened the front door for Gregor. "OK," she said, "go out and see what's happening in the cat world." She watched him pause briefly at the top of the stairs, bobbing his big head and sniffing the night air. Then he trotted down the steps and veered off to the left, heading for the communal cat track, a matted-down pathway that snaked through the grass along the side of the house and continued on through Mr. Nettlebury's back yard next door. All the neighborhood cats followed the same route.

It was drizzling lightly, and the air smelled clean and fresh. Margit took a deep breath and stared for a moment at the dark, silent houses across the street. Everyone else was safe in bed, fully intending to sleep as late as possible on this Sunday morning. There was no traffic, and the harsh light cast by the tall streetlamp on the corner gave the whole neighborhood the look of a stage set. Margit felt suddenly disoriented and queasy, as if she were staring at a life-size version of a Magritte painting—the one of a perfectly normal, dark nighttime street with a perversely unnatural blue sky and sunlit clouds overhead. She didn't dare look up.

The piercing whistle of the kettle made Margit jump. She quickly shut the door, locked it carefully, and then went back to the kitchen.

Margit filled the teapot with boiling water, took a mug from the dish rack, and carried both of them into the dining room. She sat down at the table with a pad of paper, a couple of felt-tip pens, the runes, and a stack of photocopies from the university library in front of her.

Was it really only seven hours ago that she had dashed in the front entrance of the library like a madwoman, still frantic to escape the man in the parking garage? She had thrown herself at the arm of the turnstile blocking the way just inside the front door, and then raced across the slick marble floor, skidding smack into Lars and practically knocking him off his feet.

"Hey," he said, throwing out his arms to keep his balance, "watch out!" And then he realized that he actually knew this person who had just slammed into him. "Margit?" he said in surprise. "What's going on?"

"What are you doing here?" she countered, pressing her right hand to her chest and trying to steady her ragged breathing.

"I came to pick up Derek. He's studying for a Swedish test."

"So you've got him learning Swedish, huh?" said Margit, managing a grin. "Looks like things are getting pretty serious between the two of you."

"I guess so," replied Lars, with a slightly sheepish expression. "But what's going on with *you*? What's the big rush?"

So Margit told Lars about the man in the parking garage and her conclusion that he was the same person who had broken into her house the night before. Maybe he was the guy prowling around the agency too. Lars wanted her to call the police, but Margit adamantly refused. She could just picture Detective Tristano getting word that "Ms." Andersson was mixed up in some trouble again.

"No way," said Margit stubbornly. "I'm fine. Nothing happened. And I'm not calling the police."

"Well at least let me walk you back to your car when you're ready to leave," said Lars with a look of concern. He wasn't used to seeing Margit so flustered and agitated. She hadn't been herself lately, but he figured that any normal person would be upset if they found someone murdered.

"That would be great," said Margit, relieved that she wouldn't have to face the parking garage alone. The guy hadn't followed her into the library, but he might still be skulking around, waiting for her to go back to her car. The mere thought gave her the chills. "I just have to find a couple of books and make some Xeroxes," she told Lars. "Can you give me half an hour?"

"Sure," he said, and they agreed to meet back at the library entrance.

Margit found the books she was looking for and copied what she needed. Lars and Derek escorted her back to her car and waited patiently for her to start the engine and pull out of the parking slot. Then they waved and strolled off, hand in hand, to retrieve their own vehicle on the next level of the garage.

Margit headed back to West Seattle on Aurora, too

stressed to put up with the maniac drivers on I-5, especially on a Saturday night. When she got home, she went straight to bed and slept like a rock until the nightmare jolted her awake.

OK, she told herself, stop thinking about that. Pay attention. And she smoothed out the page of runes, which was starting to look a little crumpled, and picked up a pen.

The numbers on her lottery ticket had made her think about what Barbro had said about the runes being all mixed up. Margit's lottery numbers were always randomly selected, but Renny picked the same numbers every week, and she always insisted that they be in a particular order. She claimed that her luck depended on it.

What if the position of the runes wasn't random after all? What if the writer of the runes wasn't as ignorant about the subject as Barbro assumed? What if there was some pattern to the apparent jumble?

Margit pulled out a photocopy of the real *futhark* and wrote the number of each rune, from 1 to 24, underneath. Then she transferred the corresponding numbers to the second row of runes that Søren had sent her. She studied the resulting line-up for a long time, but couldn't make any sense of it. The numbers were not in ascending or descending order, and there wasn't a pattern of even and odd numbers or any other logical sequence. Margit sighed. It was probably a crazy idea, anyway.

She poured herself another cup of tea. And then she saw it.

If she divided up the *futhark* into the three families of eight runes each, as Barbro had explained, and she took into account that the three groups, the *ættir*, were arranged in reverse order, then there were three runes in the correct position: 22, 15, and 4.

ᛏᛒᛖᛗᚱᛜᛗᛉ ᚺᛏᛁᛋᛌᚲᚤᛋ ᚠᚢᚦᛏᚱᚲᚷᚠ
17 18 19 20 21 22 23 24   9 10 11 12 13 14 15 16   1 2 3 4 5 6 7 8

ᛗᛏᛚᚱᛜᛒᛗ ᛏᛋᛋᛌᚺᛁᚤᚲ ᚠᚨᚷᛏᚦᚢᚲᚱ
23 17 21 24 20 <u>22</u> 18 19   10 12 16 13 9 11 <u>15</u> 14   8 1 7 <u>4</u> 3 2 6 5

All of the other twenty-one runes were in the wrong place. There had to be something significant about those three numbers or the runes they represented. Margit was sure of it.

She huddled over the paper, racking her brain for some kind of explanation, but she couldn't think of a thing. She finally gave up and put the runes aside. Then she looked at the stack of photocopies she had made at the library. There were several articles about runes, as well as a lengthy essay on the Golden Horns, but she was suddenly too tired to read any of them.

Margit got up from the table, switched off the light, and trudged down the hall to the bedroom. She kicked off her moccasins and untied her bathrobe, letting it drop to the floor. Then she turned off the lamp on the nightstand and lay down on the bed, pulling the covers up to her chin. She was exhausted, and her whole body craved sleep. Margit took a deep breath and then exhaled slowly, feeling the tension starting to seep out of her muscles. She put her hands on her abdomen, noting with satisfaction that it was definitely flatter than a few months ago. Last week Joe had even teased her about jabbing himself on her sharp hip bone. Her exercise routine was really starting to pay off.

Then she rolled over onto her left side and closed her eyes. In a few minutes she was sound asleep.

⌘

At 8:15 on Sunday morning, Margit sat up in bed with a groan and decided that it was time to get up. Bad dreams had continued to plague her, and she finally had to force herself awake. Enough was enough.

In the last scene, she had been stumbling down a gauntlet of uniformed policemen lined up along a country road. All the officers were standing with their arms folded across their chests, glaring at her malevolently. They hissed and jeered as she passed, and she could feel their hot breath on her face. Off in the distance she could see two centaurs cavorting in a field. Their faces bore an uncanny resemblance to the familiar features of Lars and Derek. And next to them was Renny, spinning feverishly like a whirling dervish, her hair in long thick dreadlocks and her brown skin glistening with sweat. Margit desperately called to her friends, but they were too far away to hear her.

She reached the end of the gauntlet at last, but this was no cause for relief. A three-headed man dressed in black stood on her right, leering at her with his six squinty eyes. He had a vicious puckered scar on each cheek, and he was clutching a yowling Gregor by the tail and swinging him overhead. On her left, Detective Tristano, dressed in his neat preppy clothes, was down on all fours with his face buried in the bloody entrails of a flopping fish.

"No!" moaned Margit, yanking herself out of the nightmare into full consciousness. She jumped out of bed, put on a pair of sweatpants and a t-shirt, and laced up her bright green Converse shoes. Then she spent the next forty minutes exercising vigorously to the searing guitar of *Are You Experienced?* turned up full blast.

Two cups of strong coffee and a hot shower erased any lingering traces of Margit's bad dreams. And the note she found from Joe in her fax machine cheered her up considerably. "Working on a new piece, will be out of touch for a few days," it said. "Miss you fiercely." And underneath he had added a meticulous line drawing of the two of them in bed, their naked bodies twisted into an impossible position, surpassing even the wildest contortions in the *Kama Sutra.* Margit laughed and scribbled a reply: "Miss you too, let's try that next time."

Then she got dressed, noting with pleasure that the sun was breaking through the clouds. It would only take her a couple of hours to finish that translation job, and then maybe she could go for a walk—or better yet, get out her new bicycle and ride down to the beach at Alki.

After a quick breakfast of fruit and low-fat granola, Margit sat down in her study and dialed the number that Søren's sister had given the funeral director. It was ten o'clock, Seattle time, which made it seven p.m. in Århus. She hoped Karin was home.

There was a crackling on the line and then a series of sharp "doots." Finally someone picked up the receiver and Margit heard a soft voice say clearly, "Karin Fønsgård."

"*Goddag,*" said Margit, glad that the connection was good and she wouldn't have to deal with the intercontinental echo that could be so disconcerting. "This is Margit Andersson in Seattle. Mr. Sanders gave me your phone number and said that you'd like me to call." She was careful to use the formal and more polite form of "you," even though it was fast dying out in modern Danish speech.

"Oh yes," said Karin. "Yes. It's so kind of you to call, Fru Andersson. I wanted to have the opportunity to thank you for befriending my brother." Her voice had that slight Jutland drawl to it, which Margit always found so charming, compared to the high-speed mumble of people from Copenhagen.

"I'm so sorry about Søren," said Margit. "I didn't know him well, but I translated a few letters for him, and I liked him a lot. He was a good person, and he certainly didn't deserve such a terrible death."

There was a pause, and then Karin said quietly, "I appreciate your sympathy, Fru Andersson. Søren wrote to me about how you helped him after his accident. And then the police told me that you were the one who found him."

"Yes," replied Margit, "I did," hoping that she wouldn't be asked to describe the scene. She didn't think she could bear it.

"I was afraid that something like this would happen to Søren," continued Karin with a sigh.

"You were?" said Margit, greatly surprised. Søren seemed to her the least likely person to end up murdered. He was a crotchety old guy who liked to fish and build weird-looking boats out of milk cartons. He had a few drinking buddies, and occasionally he went over to the neighborhood senior center when he wanted a hot meal and didn't feel like cooking. Otherwise he kept pretty much to himself. And there was certainly nothing in his junk-filled house that would be worth stealing.

"I've had this funny feeling about him ever since the war," Karin told Margit. "I can't really explain it—I was only a teenager at the time. But when Søren came back home from the army

113

after the Germans invaded South Jutland and then occupied all of Denmark in 1940, there was something very strange about him. He seemed different, and I don't think it was just the shock of the war—although he never talked much about that, either. He was with the Tønder garrison, one of the few outfits to offer any resistance when the Germans poured across the border. Only eleven Danes were killed, but some of Søren's friends were among them."

"What do you mean by 'different'?" asked Margit.

"He practically stopped talking, and he spent all of his time with his nose buried in dusty old books. He'd never been much of a reader before. He seemed withdrawn and preoccupied, but when I asked him what he was studying, he refused to tell me. He would give me an odd look and then shut himself up in his room. I couldn't understand it. He'd never been a secretive person before. He was my fun-loving big brother, and he always used to tease me and pull my braids. Suddenly he seemed like a stranger in the house."

"Are you sure it wasn't just the tension of the war? A lot of people must have gone kind of crazy during the occupation."

"No, that wasn't it. Everybody was anxious and afraid, but Søren was obsessed. It wasn't normal, not even for those terrible times. He was completely changed. After the war he made his living as a fisherman, and he seemed more and more peculiar the older he got. He was paranoid about strangers, and he kept his house locked up all the time. Nobody else locked their doors in that small town where he lived. I felt sorry for Søren. He was jumpy and nervous, and he always seemed to be looking over his shoulder. He never married, and he hardly had any friends."

"But then he moved to the States," said Margit.

"Yes, our younger brother Ole was living over there. He died in 1975. He was a widower with no children, so he left his house in Seattle to Søren. I was surprised that Søren was suddenly so eager to leave Denmark. He didn't even speak much English back then, but he didn't waste any time. He just packed up his bags and moved."

"And he never returned to Denmark for a visit?" asked Margit, even though she knew the answer.

"No," said Karin sadly. "I never saw him again." There was a pause and then she continued. "I kept trying to get him to come back, though. Especially after I started getting the postcards."

"What postcards?" said Margit.

"Well, about a year ago, Søren wrote and told me that he had given my address to a friend, and he said that if he got any letters at my house, I was supposed to forward them right away. I thought this was a little odd, but as I said, Søren was a peculiar man, and it never did any good to ask for explanations. One day a letter did arrive addressed to him, and so I sent it on to Seattle. I didn't think much more about it until a postcard arrived a few months later, also addressed to Søren. I couldn't help reading it, of course."

"What did it say?" asked Margit.

"It said: 'Still waiting for your reply.' That's all. No signature and no return address. I put it in an envelope and forwarded it to Søren. A month later another card arrived, and it said, 'Urgent that we meet.' After a third one came, I started getting a little nervous. That one didn't sound so friendly. It said: 'You are playing a dangerous game.'"

"Then what happened?" asked Margit.

"I wrote to Søren and asked him what it was all about, but he told me it was nothing. Three more postcards came, but they had no message on them, just his name and my address. That gave me a bad feeling—I didn't like it at all. So I started urging Søren to come back to Denmark. I thought he ought to go to the Danish police and get their help with this matter, whatever it was. But he wouldn't listen to me. And he finally forbade me ever to mention the topic again. I just knew something bad was going to happen. And now he's dead."

"Do you still have any of those postcards, Fru Fønsgård?" asked Margit.

"No, I sent them all to Søren. And I never want to see that picture again as long as I live."

"What picture?"

"Didn't I tell you?" said Karin. "The postcards were from the Silkeborg Museum and they were all exactly the same. That's why I remember them so well. They all had a picture of the Tollund man on them."

"My God," gasped Margit, instantly envisioning the dark leathery skin and closed eyes of that ancient man whose body had been thrown into the Danish bogs over two thousand years ago. She remembered reading that in the early 1950s he had been pulled out of his peat grave near Tollund, and his miraculously intact head had been put on display in a museum in Jutland.

Margit also remembered reading that the Tollund man had been hanged—killed as a sacrifice to the Spring.

10

After the startling phone conversation with Søren's sister, Margit decided to take her bike ride first and work on the horticultural translation later in the day. She needed to get out of the house.

She stuffed her wallet, a scarf, and an extra sweater into a daypack and strapped on her bicycle helmet. She missed feeling the wind blowing through her hair, but she had read all the horror stories about head injuries suffered in bicycle accidents. And these days everybody seemed so impatient and irritable when they got behind the wheel of a car—bike riders were just an added nuisance on the road. Margit had to admit that the new helmet law was a good idea.

She locked the front door and went around the side of the house to get her bicycle out of the garage. Gregor trotted along beside her, clearly intent on sneaking inside and hiding out among the lawn furniture, boxes of unwanted records and dishes, and bags of carefully folded old clothes. It was the only place in the house where Margit allowed her slight pack-rat tendency to take over. Every couple of years, she would haul everything off to the Goodwill or the dump, and for a few months the Mazda would reclaim its rightful place in the garage. Then things would start to pile up, and the car would be relegated once again to a parking spot in the driveway.

Gregor wound his way in between a pile of discarded drapes and a teetering stack of jigsaw puzzles, but Margit was quite familiar with Gregor's game, and she chased him out before closing the garage door. Then she hopped on her shiny blue mountain bike and headed down to Alki.

The sunny weather had brought everyone out, and the path along the beach was crowded with joggers, rollerbladers, and people walking their dogs. Margit pedaled slowly, staring out over the Sound at the snow-capped mountains, nodding to the familiar twin peaks of The Brothers, and trying in vain to catch a glimpse of Mt. Olympus. The view was so spectacular that she almost didn't mind the hubbub of insistent voices ebbing and flowing around her.

Sometimes Margit wished she had the power of an old-time movie director to screech "quiet on the set" into a megaphone and receive utter obedience from everyone in sight. Sometimes she wondered how all these people could keep up their incessant and inane chatter in the face of such incredible natural beauty.

Weren't they ever stunned into silence? Hadn't they ever been struck dumb by the radiance of a sunset or the sight of a perfect "V" of Canada geese flying overhead? Sometimes she wondered why people bothered to leave their houses at all.

Three hours later Margit was back in front of her computer. She read her e-mail before starting to work and found a message from Barbro Ólafsdóttir.

"Can you meet me at the museum library around seven tonight? Found something that might interest you."

"OK," Margit typed in reply. "Meet you at the main entrance." The Nordic Heritage Museum closed at four o'clock on Sunday, so Barbro would have to come down to open the door. She must be planning to work late.

There was also an e-mail message from Liisa, requesting all the freelancers to be at the agency for a ten o'clock meeting on Monday morning. Margit sighed. She had been hoping to dash in, deliver her job, and make a quick getaway. Now she was going to get stuck listening to Liisa's latest harangue, whatever it was this time, for at least an hour.

Margit answered a few other messages before finally deciding that she had procrastinated long enough. She had to finish that translation. Methodically she set to work, but half her mind was still thinking about what Karin had said.

When the last sentence was finally translated, Margit saved her file, copied it to a backup disk, and turned off her computer. Then she headed straight for the basement library, found a book by Palle Lauring on the history of Denmark, and sat down to read about the Tollund man.

The book said that back in the early Iron Age, the Danes often tossed swords, shields, and other spoils of war into the sacred marshes as a sacrifice to the gods of battle. They also consigned human sacrifices to the peat bogs in an appeal for a bountiful spring. The Danish soil possessed a peculiar mixture of chemicals that tanned the skin of the corpses and preserved them for thousands of years in remarkably whole condition.

The Tollund man was the most famous of these victims. Even the contents of his stomach were still intact, and scientists were able to determine that his last meal had consisted of a porridge made from barley, flaxseed, and knotgrass.

Margit gagged at the thought of such a meal and looked again at the photograph of the Tollund man. His hair was close-cropped under the peaked leather cap he was wearing. A slight stubble was visible on his lean, leathery cheeks. He had deep furrows on his forehead, wrinkles under his eyes, and his closed eyelids were heavily creased. But his expression was amazingly calm, almost serene—as if he were merely asleep. Around his neck was the braided strap that had taken his life. Margit had to admit that it was a very eerie picture, and she could certainly understand why Karin Fønsgård had been upset by its repeated appearance on the postcards arriving for Søren.

The Tollund man was clearly an ominous warning that Søren had been unwilling or unable to heed.

Margit turned back to her book and read the rest of the chapter, sitting up straight with a start when she got to the last page. It said that in 1863 a fabulous find was made in the bogs at Nydam in South Jutland: two large boats and an entire cache of ancient weapons. A year later, the Danes and the Germans were at war, and a wide swath of South Jutland was lost to Germany, and with it the valuable find. "And to this day, the treasures remain in Schleswig," Margit read.

Seventy-six years later the Germans overran Denmark again, and Karin had said that Søren was then a soldier in South Jutland.

What if Søren knew about the previous loss of priceless artifacts to the Germans? What if he had discovered something valuable himself? What if he wanted to protect it from the invaders?

And after the war, what if he decided to keep it?

That might explain his odd behavior and the increasing paranoia that Karin had mentioned. Margit could imagine the mixture of excitement and anxiety that possession of such a treasure would evoke. She could almost picture a much younger version of the Søren she had known, crouching down in a dim corner of his house and taking some carefully wrapped object out of its hiding place. She could see him folding back the soft cloth and staring at what he held in his hands, an expression of reverence and awe on his face. But the secret must have weighed on him terribly.

Søren had probably made the right decision to say nothing about it during the long years of the occupation, but how could he justify his reasons for concealing it when the threat of war had passed? How could he admit to his own covetous greed in keeping a national treasure all to himself?

No doubt Søren had settled on his own excuses for continuing his exclusive guardianship. No doubt he had decided that this object, whatever it was, would be safer in his hands than in some museum or private art collection, which were always subject to theft, no matter how extensive their security systems.

If Margit was right, it was no wonder that Søren kept his door locked and was suspicious of strangers. It was no wonder he had few friends and grew more and more eccentric over the years. And it was easy to understand why he would jump at the chance to move as far away from Denmark as possible, taking both his secret and his guilt along with him.

Margit closed her book, put it back on the shelf, and slowly climbed the basement stairs to the kitchen. She put a pot of water on the stove and then stood leaning against the fridge, mulling over her theory about Søren. The boiling water finally caught her attention and she absentmindedly threw in half a package of rotini. When the pasta was ready, she dished up a plateful, added a dab of margarine and a sprinkling of parmesan, and sat down at the dining-room table.

The photocopies from the university library were still there, and Margit skimmed through the article about the Golden Horns as she ate. Halfway through her dinner, she dropped her fork onto the glass plate with a loud clang. She read the passage again in disbelief.

It said that it was common hearsay around Gallehus in South Jutland that in 1830 a third horn was found close to the site of the other discoveries. And that the finder of this horn had shamelessly sold it in Hamburg, where it was eventually melted down. The story had never been verified, however.

Margit leaned back against the hard spindles of the chair, her mind reeling. Imagine *three* priceless horns, each found roughly a century apart, and in approximately the same location.

And then she remembered another passage that she had just read in the Lauring history book. In the section right before the Tollund man, there was a paragraph about other items found buried in the Danish bogs. Among them were dozens of bronze *lurs*, ancient wind instruments over a meter long. They were strange-looking things, consisting of a thin curved pipe with a mouthpiece at one end and an ornamental plate encircling the opening at the other. But the most striking thing about these *lurs* was that they were always found in pairs.

Margit took a deep breath, trying to control her excitement.

Two Golden Horns discovered and then irretrievably lost. A third horn also reported found and destroyed.

What if the horns, like the *lurs*, always occurred in pairs? What if there was a fourth Golden Horn?

⌘

Margit pulled up outside the Nordic Heritage Museum with a screech and turned off the engine. She was appallingly late—it was almost eight o'clock—and it was all the fault of her wretched vehicle. She had left West Seattle in plenty of time to meet Barbro by seven, but the Mazda had decided not to cooperate. Margit gave the steering wheel an angry thump with her fist.

The car had been giving her a lot of trouble lately, refusing to start until the eighth or ninth try, and then stalling whenever she came to a full stop. She had gotten into the habit of shifting into neutral at every red light, which seemed to be the only way to keep the idle above a thousand rpm. It usually did the trick, but tonight the Mazda had stopped dead at an intersection on Elliott Avenue, and she finally had to call AAA to get it jump-started. God only knew whether she'd be able to drive the car home. Margit promised herself to take it to the shop the next day. It definitely needed a tune-up.

She had tried several times to call Barbro from her car phone to explain her tardiness, but each time she got the museum's recording. Margit finally left a message on the answering machine without much hope that Barbro would listen to it. By this time, she had probably given up and gone back to work, or maybe even left for home. Margit would have to stand outside the library window and yell to get Barbro's attention, if she was still there. She just hoped that the neighbors across the street wouldn't notice all the shouting.

Margit slammed the car door and ran up the stairs toward the museum. She hurried around the side of the building, deciding to check the main entrance to see whether Barbro had left her a note. She found the door standing wide open.

"Barbro?" said Margit loudly as she stepped across the threshold. "Sorry I'm late. My car was acting up again, and I had to call AAA to get it jumped." She expected to find Barbro sitting at the reception desk, absorbed in a book, but the lobby was deserted. "Barbro?" called Margit again.

Everything looked perfectly normal: the lights were all on, the three chairs were primly lined up behind the desk, and the catalogs and flyers on the table were neatly stacked. There was a sprig of forsythia in a slender glass vase on the counter next to the elevator, and the clock on the wall was ticking quietly.

But something was wrong. Margit could feel it. The air seemed charged with an excess of electricity. She suddenly felt tense and on edge.

Margit turned around to pull the heavy front door closed, making sure that it locked. She didn't need someone sneaking up behind her. Then she slowly surveyed the lobby again, letting her eyes rest on each object, one at a time, looking for anything odd or out of place. And she finally found it.

The brightly lit hallway on her left served as a small gallery, and the current show was a collection of lithographs by a Saami artist. One of the prints was hanging wildly askew.

The hallway was also the entrance to the popular exhibit,

"The Dream of America," a series of interconnected rooms illustrating the Scandinavian immigrant experience in full-scale sets. It was ingeniously designed to make the spectators feel as if they were actually setting out across the ocean and then stepping ashore in the new land. Margit had seen the exhibit several times, marveling at the authenticity of every detail.

The crooked print seemed to point in that direction, so Margit took a deep breath and then headed stealthily down the hallway. She turned the corner and entered the first room.

She was standing on the wharf of some small coastal town in turn-of-the-century Norway or Sweden. She could hear the steady trickling of the water under the thick boards of the dock, and in the bluish light of the pre-dawn set, she could see the hull of a white-sided ship looming up before her. Margit cautiously climbed a short flight of stairs and found herself standing on the deck of the steamer that was about to carry a brave contingency of immigrants to a faraway land. Bulky crates, battered trunks, and coils of rough rope were piled up on the deck. Margit moved over to the railing and looked out at the view of an endless sea. A wooden lifeboat hung overhead, suspended from its davit.

A sudden loud clank made Margit whirl around to stare into the shadows on the deck, adrenaline surging through her body. She felt disoriented, and she couldn't tell where the noise had come from. Nothing moved. Then a hair-raising creak followed by a scuffling sound sent her racing down the stairs to the wharf, headed for the exit.

But the sound of her own name stopped Margit in her tracks. She turned around to look back at the ship, and there was Barbro peering down at her from inside the elevated lifeboat.

"Margit!" exclaimed Barbro again. "Thank God you're here." She took a firm grip on the gunwale, and with a graceful vault she landed solidly on her feet on the deck below. "Did you see anybody in the building? Is he still here?"

"Who?" whispered Margit, wide-eyed and flushed, her breathing uneven with fear. She blinked rapidly. Barbro's sudden emergence was so incongruous that Margit almost thought she was looking at an apparition.

"The guy who was after me," said Barbro, smoothing back her hair with her right hand. There was a big rip in the sleeve of her black Los Lobos sweatshirt. "I came down to open the door for you at seven, and there was this man hanging around the entrance. I told him the museum was closed, but he said he had to talk to me. He said it was about some runes. I told him to come back on Tuesday when the library was open, but he said it couldn't wait. I didn't like the looks of him, so I was just about to close the door in his face when he pulls out a knife and barges right in."

"What did you do?" gasped Margit, putting her hand on a post at the edge of the wharf, hoping to regain her equilibrium by touching something solid.

"I backed up toward the reception desk, thinking that I'd make a try for the phone, but no such luck. He motioned me over to the other side of the lobby and told me not to try anything if I didn't want to get hurt. He said he just wanted to ask me some questions."

"What did he want to know?" asked Margit, guessing what Barbro would say.

"He asked me whether anyone had been over recently to

show me some runes. When I said no, he told me to quit playing games. And then he mentioned your name."

"I thought he would. Did he have scratches on his face?"

"Yes, as a matter of fact, he did. How did you know?" asked Barbro.

"My cat attacked a man who broke into my house on Friday night. I'm pretty sure he was looking for those runes I showed you. So I thought it might be the same guy. Then what happened?"

"I told him I didn't know what he was talking about. That really made him mad, and he started waving his knife around. When he got close enough to slash my sleeve, I decided I had to take action. So I kicked him in the balls." Barbro grinned and stuck out her right foot toward Margit, wiggling the pointed toe of her cowboy boot.

"Wow," said Margit appreciatively, picturing the scene. "You're amazing."

"Not really," Barbro said modestly. "My brothers taught me how to fight and I'm not afraid of bullies, but I don't like knives. So I had to resort to more extreme measures." And she nodded with satisfaction. "He was blocking the way to the door, so I ran down the hallway and in here to the exhibit rooms. I knew I couldn't outrun him, so I looked around for a good hiding place."

"How on earth did you ever get up there?" asked Margit, staring at the lifeboat hanging at least six feet in the air.

"I'm good at gymnastics," said Barbro with a laugh. "Keeps me in shape. I'm just glad the boat was solidly attached. I thought my weight might bring it crashing to the deck."

Barbro reached up to pat the underside of the lifeboat approvingly. Then she went on with her story.

"I heard him come into the room and walk around for a while, so I just laid low. It was a big relief when you showed up. How long have I been here, anyway?"

"It's past eight," Margit told her. "But how did you know it was me? How come you didn't think it was the guy with the knife?"

"Your perfume," said Barbro. "That citrusy scent you always wear. I knew it had to be you."

"My soap," said Margit, deciding at once to switch to a less pungent brand. "I never wear perfume."

Then Barbro came down the steps to the wharf and gave Margit a hug of gratitude.

"Come on," she said, "let's go back to the lobby and call the cops."

"OK," Margit agreed, realizing that this time things had gone too far. They were going to have to report the incident to the police.

"By the way," Barbro said as they entered the lobby and walked over to the reception desk, "I think I know who the guy with the knife is."

And then she laughed heartily at Margit's look of astonishment and refused to say another word about it until after she had called the police.

11

The freelancers of the Koivisto Translation Agency were crowded around the long teak table in the conference room on Monday morning, restlessly waiting for Liisa to finish her speech. She had been talking nonstop for forty-five minutes and was still plunging ahead full steam. It looked as if they were going to be there for at least another half hour. They weren't actually obligated to show up, since only the full-time staff members got paid for the meeting, but they all liked to stay on good terms with Liisa. Freelancers were always nervous about where their next job was coming from.

Margit glanced over at Lars, who was sitting across from her, and rolled her eyes. He smiled, pushed up his glasses, and yawned demonstratively. Then he took another sip of coffee from the styrofoam cup in front of him.

Yuri was fiddling with an oversized paper clip, twisting it into little animal shapes, smoothing it out flat, and then starting all over again. Jennifer was slouched in her chair with her arms crossed and her eyes closed, a half-eaten bagel and a china teacup sitting in a little puddle of water on the table in front of her.

Margit didn't know most of the other freelancers, except by name, since they all worked so much at home.

Tony, the Spanish translator, was leaning back with his hands behind his head and his eyes fixed on the ceiling. Raymond was quietly tapping a persistent staccato beat on the tabletop, and Ursula was staring out the window with a bored look on her face, twisting a lock of hair around her right forefinger. Everyone else was in a similar state of dazed impatience, letting the rush of Liisa's words wash over them.

Every couple of months Liisa would call a meeting to "bring everyone up to date," as she said. She was under the illusion that they were all as keenly interested in the financial projections and long-term plans for the agency as she was. The business was her passion, and she seemed to spend every waking hour on the phone with clients, going over completed translations, or running off to appointments to rustle up more work. Margit was surprised to learn that Liisa actually had a family— a stockbroker husband and two teenage sons. She wondered when they ever spent any time together.

The meetings all followed a predictable course. Liisa would start off with a brisk run-down of new clients and then move on to a rapid-fire account of all the big jobs the agency had brought in recently. She would go over the usual housekeeping complaints, inevitably reminding everybody to turn off any lights and computers not in use—the electric bill was always too high, in her opinion.

The second half of her speech would be reserved for an intense tirade on some subject, which was the real reason for the meeting.

Today the chosen topic was building security, and Margit ducked when she heard her own name mentioned in connection with the break-in the previous week. She just hoped Liisa wasn't going to go into detail about her ignominious exit through the back window.

"And so I've decided to install a new card-key system for the office," Liisa was saying. "It's an enormous expense, but a necessary one, and after investigating a number of options, I've decided that this is the best solution." Then Liisa launched into a tedious description of the pros and cons of various high-tech security systems, and Margit simply tuned out.

She put her chin on her hand and stared at the polished tabletop, thinking about her conversation with Barbro and the police the night before.

⌘

Barbro's call to 911 brought two uniformed police officers to the museum in less than ten minutes. They made a quick search of the building to reassure themselves that the assailant was not still hiding somewhere. Then Barbro suggested that they sit in the library, and when they were all settled around one of the study tables, the police asked Margit and Barbro a number of questions.

They were just finishing up their report when one of the officers got a call, and he excused himself and left the room. He returned to the library a few minutes later with a rather cranky-looking Detective Tristano behind him. He was wearing the same neat blue blazer and khaki pants, but Margit was surprised to see that his shirt was badly wrinkled and his tie was loose.

"Well, *Ms.* Andersson," said the detective, careful to emphasize her proper title. "You certainly seem to be attracting a lot of attention lately. I didn't expect to see you again so soon." He sounded thoroughly annoyed.

"It's not my favorite way to spend a Sunday night, either," snapped Margit, instantly riled. "What's the matter, did we drag you away from your little love nest or something?"

Barbro gave her a startled glance, but Margit was shamelessly delighted to see the detective blush. "Touché," she murmured. She had finally found a way to crack his confident veneer.

"OK, Ned," said Detective Tristano, turning to one of the officers who was trying not to smirk, "what exactly happened here?" He pulled up a chair and sat down to listen to the report.

After he heard the whole story, the detective turned to Margit and said tersely, "Let's see those runes, Ms. Andersson."

She reluctantly handed over the crumpled piece of paper, glad that she had made herself a copy, which was still safely inside her bag. She expected to hear another speech about civic obligations and obstructing the investigation, but the detective managed to restrain himself this time.

"What are these numbers underneath?" he asked, noting the numerals written in blue ink. "Did you put them there?"

"Yes, I did," said Margit, and she explained her theory about the three runes being in the correct position. She wasn't going to mention her run-in with the assailant at the university parking garage, but otherwise she figured there was no use in keeping back anything else from the police. Things had gotten way out of hand, and she would rather let the cops do the detective work. She had had enough excitement for one week.

Detective Tristano took out a small leather-bound notebook and made a few notes with a silver ballpoint pen. Then he carefully folded up the runes and handed the paper to the police officer sitting next to him, who slipped it into an envelope for safekeeping. The detective gave Margit a stern look but didn't say anything more about the runes. Then he asked Barbro to repeat her description of the man with the knife.

"About five-nine, thin and wiry, maybe a hundred and fifty pounds. In his late thirties. Short brown hair, blue eyes, clean-shaven, a couple of big scratches on his left cheek," recited Barbro. "He was wearing a jean jacket over a dark turtleneck, black pants, and brown leather driving gloves."

"You've got a remarkable memory," said the detective. "Most witnesses aren't that precise."

"I'm a detail person," Barbro told him. "It's necessary in my field."

"So do you remember what kind of knife he had?" asked Detective Tristano. "Can you describe it?"

"A nasty-looking switchblade," said Barbro, giving Margit a wink. "Not something you'd want to fool around with."

"Anything else you can tell us about him, Ms. Ólafsdóttir? Was there anything unusual about the man?"

"Well, he seemed awfully jittery, really high-strung. Especially for a Dane."

"What makes you think he was a Dane?" asked Detective Tristano with surprise.

"His accent," said Barbro. "Didn't I mention that before? He had a very distinct Danish accent."

"Anything else? Are you sure you don't remember anything else about him? Now think carefully," persisted the detective.

"That's about it," said Barbro. "It wasn't exactly a social

occasion, and I didn't have much time to ask him questions."

Apparently the detective's humorless and brusque manner was having its effect on Barbro as well, and she was starting to lose her patience. Margit wondered what kind of woman would put up with that patronizing tone of his. But maybe he was great in bed.

"I'll tell you one thing, though," said Barbro, "I'm pretty sure I know who the guy is." And she sat back in her chair with a smug expression, enjoying the look of utter amazement on the faces of the three police officers. She'd been saving up her trump card for the right dramatic moment.

"What do you mean?" asked Detective Tristano. "Who is he?"

"Well, I can't tell you his name," said Barbro, "but I think he's a collector. And probably the same one who made a spectacular purchase at Sotheby's a few years back. A hundred thousand dollars for a tiny gold coin called a pagoda. Sold to an anonymous buyer through an intermediary."

"I don't get it," said the detective. "What's the connection?"

"OK," said Barbro, "now listen carefully."

Margit smiled at her intended gibe.

"I've been thinking about the lost Golden Horns ever since Margit showed me the runes and told me about the matching sketches. So I did a little investigating on my own and discovered a reference to a pagoda 'made from the stolen Golden Horns' in an old auction catalog dating from 1809. Apparently an attempt was made to track down this coin in the 1920s, but to no avail. I wondered whether it had ever turned up again, so I sent off an e-mail on the Internet to a colleague at the Royal Library in Copenhagen. This morning I got a reply."

Barbro paused for a good thirty seconds, prompting Detective Tristano to ask impatiently, "And?"

"And she told me that the coin did show up again, at an auction in 1987, along with its original bill of sale from none other than Niels Heidenreich."

"That was the thief who stole the Golden Horns?" asked the detective, clearly struggling to keep the whole story straight. Margit suspected that he wasn't used to homicide cases that required him to follow up on leads over three centuries old.

"Yes," said Barbro. "And my colleague faxed me a copy of the document. I made another copy for you. Just a second."

Barbro got up from the table and went over to her desk, where she rummaged through the stacks of papers for a minute until she found what she was looking for.

"Here it is," she said, handing the page to Margit as she sat down again. "I'll let the professional translator do the honors."

Margit quickly scanned the Danish and then translated it for the police:

> I, the undersigned, have sold to my lord, Mister Anders Vestergaard, a pair of gold shoe buckles, as well as one gold pagoda, the legitimate acquisition of which I do in all manner vouch for; and for his assurance I have issued him this certificate signed by my own hand.
>
> Copenhagen, the 10th of June 1802.
>
> Signed: N. Heidenreich, Watchmaker, residing at the corner of Studiestræde and Lille Larsbjørnstræde, No. 105, on the ground floor.

"Thanks," said Barbro, taking the paper from Margit and handing it to Detective Tristano. "Apparently it was common practice back then for goldsmiths to issue this type of certificate. It was supposed to protect the buyer from prosecution if the gold turned out to be the property of someone else. Like the king of Denmark, for instance."

"And you said this coin was auctioned off at Sotheby's?" asked the detective.

"That's right," Barbro replied. "According to my colleague, the coin was put up for sale in 1987 when the estate of a wealthy German count was dispersed. Even though it couldn't be proved that the gold had originally come from the stolen horns, the accompanying certificate was judged to be authentic. And certain documents found among the papers of the late count verified the path of the coin from the possession of the aforementioned Anders Vestergaard to the 1809 auction and onward—until it finally ended up with the German count."

"So the gold counterfeit coin came to Sotheby's with a legitimate pedigree, based on the signature of a thief," said Margit, struck by the irony of the situation.

"Yes," said Barbro. "Incredible, isn't it? The coin wasn't flashy enough to get much media attention, but it caused quite a stir among collectors. My colleague says that the Danish government tried to claim ownership, but the German heirs just laughed and said the bidding was open to anyone with sufficient funds. And I guess the final price must have been too steep for the Danish authorities, because the coin was sold to a private collector—anonymous, as I said."

"And you think this collector is the same person who threatened you with a knife tonight?" The detective sounded skeptical. "Why would someone rich enough to spend a hundred thousand dollars on a single coin run all over Seattle breaking into buildings and maybe even murder an old man? Why wouldn't he get someone else to do his dirty work?"

"Have you ever met a collector?" asked Barbro quietly. "I mean a *real* collector—someone who is rabid about rare gems or stamps or coins? They're fanatics and extremely cunning about getting what they want. I have a cousin who collects baseball cards, and even on his limited income he doesn't think twice about paying a hundred bucks for some new addition to his collection. He puts each card in a special plastic sleeve, and he won't let anybody touch his stuff—keeps everything locked up tight in a safe in the bedroom. That's just on a small scale compared to the high-rollers who collect really valuable things. Like ancient artifacts, for instance. And the higher the stakes, the more paranoid these people get. I don't think this guy would trust anyone with what he's looking for."

"And what is that?" asked Detective Tristano, sounding exasperated. He had no patience for the wild theories of ordinary citizens, who usually got all their ideas about murders from lurid TV shows. He'd been involved in plenty of homicide cases, and the stories behind them were usually a lot more mundane and a lot less complicated than this bizarre tale he was listening to.

"What do you think the guy's looking for?" he asked again.

"Another Golden Horn," said Margit. "He's after the fourth Golden Horn."

⌘

At 11:45 Margit stomped out of the agency and ran down the stairs in a truly foul mood. The freelancer meeting had lasted well over an hour. When Liisa finally summed up her remarks and told everyone they could get back to work, the room cleared out in a matter of seconds. But Liisa caught up with Margit in the front office as she was heading toward the door and handed her another rush job, due by eleven the next morning. Margit took one look at the wad of Danish financial documents and gave the folder back to her boss.

"Sorry, but I can't do it," she said firmly. "You know accounting isn't my strong point, and you've never been happy with my translations of financial reports. Have you asked Lars?"

"Lars is still tied up with that Swedish computer manual. He doesn't have time for this," said Liisa, handing the folder back.

"No, really, I can't do it," Margit protested. "I worked all weekend and I haven't had a day off since I got back from vacation." Except for the day I found Søren, she thought to herself, but that didn't really count and she wasn't going to bring it up.

"Come on, Margit," said Liisa, "this job isn't so hard. It's not really accounting language, anyway. I looked at it myself and it's perfectly straightforward prose. And besides, there's nobody else who can do it." Then Liisa spun around and dashed off down the hall, her red skirt swirling and her high heels clicking on the hardwood floor.

Margit stuffed the folder into her briefcase in disgust, receiving a sympathetic look from Hannah, the receptionist, who had witnessed this kind of scene a thousand times before in her nine years with the agency. It was impossible to argue with Liisa.

"I do *not* have time for this today," muttered Margit angrily as she pushed open the front door of the building and stepped out onto Second Avenue. It was a cold gray day with a brisk wind that whipped Margit's blonde hair into her face. She stopped in the middle of the sidewalk to put down her briefcase and pull her hair into a ponytail, twisting an elastic band around it. Then she turned up the collar of her jacket and put on a pair of wool gloves.

The weather was always so unpredictable at this time of year. Yesterday she was riding her bike along the beach in brilliant sunshine, wishing she had worn shorts instead of jeans. But today it felt just like November.

Margit picked up her briefcase and walked over to First Avenue, heading toward the Seattle Art Museum. She had promised to pick up the new Jacob Lawrence book for Renny at the museum store, and then she had to catch a bus out to the U District to reclaim the Mazda. She had left it at Ralston Automotive on NE 65th Street (the only mechanic in town she trusted) before coming in for the morning meeting at the agency. It was just Margit's luck that Liisa would give her this lousy job on a day when she was without wheels. That translation was going to take her at least nine hours, but she wouldn't be able to get started until late afternoon. It was going to be a long night, Margit realized with a sigh.

She found the art museum closed—she had forgotten it was Monday—so she turned up the street toward the entrance of the bus tunnel at Second and University. The lunchtime crowds were bending into the wind, their shoulders hunched and their hands clutching their coat collars closed. It had started

to rain, but umbrellas were completely useless in this wind—
everyone was resigned to getting wet.

Margit walked swiftly along the diagonal dirt path lined
with rough-cut blocks of granite. The city had finally given up
on trying to direct pedestrians along the paved pathway laid out
perpendicular to the sidewalk. From the first day the tunnel
opened, everyone had cut diagonally across the grass until there
was a well-worn track on either side of the official path.

Margit glanced briefly at the scrubby slopes surrounding
the entrance and the rusty orange girders framing the doorway.
She always wondered why this station had such an ugly and un-
finished look, while all the other tunnel entrances were fixed up
so snazzy. Margit pulled open the glass door and stepped inside,
grateful to be out of the rain and biting wind. She turned left and
headed toward the stairway leading down to the bus bay for
northbound traffic.

As she put her foot on the top step, a man came up next to
her, leaned close, and snarled in Danish, "Give me that goddamn piece of paper."

Margit turned her head, startled, and looked straight into
the furious blue eyes of the man with the scratches on his face.

12

I don't know what you're talking about," said Margit feebly, tearing her eyes away from the man's scratched left cheek and forcing herself to look straight ahead. Her heart was pounding so loudly that she could barely hear her own voice. She held her briefcase tightly in her left hand as they moved down the stairs, side by side.

"You know perfectly well what I'm talking about. I'm through playing games with you, and I want that paper with the runes."

Margit looked down toward the platform below, thinking she might be able to make a run for it, but the man seemed to read her mind and gripped her right elbow hard.

"Don't do anything rash," he hissed. "I've got a knife, and you know I won't hesitate to use it. One quick jab and you'd be a goner, just like somebody else you know."

Margit inhaled sharply.

"All I want is the paper with the runes. I'm not going to hurt you if you give me what I want. So hand it over." He gave her elbow an impatient squeeze.

Margit had her doubts that this man would let her off so easily, even if she did give up her copy of the runes. His whole body was crackling with tension, and he had practically admitted to one murder and then threatened her with her own. His desperation and greed had obviously gotten the better of him, and he had finally thrown all caution aside by deciding to confront her in such a public place. He must have followed her from the agency in Belltown.

"OK," she said bitterly. "You're right. I did have the paper with the runes, but I gave it to the police. Last night after you tried to stab my friend at the museum."

"You're lying," he seethed as they reached the bottom of the stairs and walked slowly along the platform. "And even if you did give it to the police, you'd have a copy. I know you would. Now where is it?" And he shook her elbow hard.

Margit was suddenly seized by a terrible impulse to laugh at the sheer absurdity of the whole situation. It was classic film noir. Here she was standing on a dimly-lit bus platform in an underground tunnel, her arm gripped tightly by a man with a concealed weapon who was threatening to knock her off if she didn't come up with the goods. He was wearing a black raincoat with the collar turned up, and it looked as if he had forgotten to shave that morning. His blue eyes were narrowed, his mouth was set in a grim line, and the vivid scratches on his cheek gave him a sinister look. The only thing missing from his villainous guise was a fedora with a tilted brim to shadow his face.

And none of the bored bystanders paid the slightest bit of attention to them, unable to understand a single word of their conversation in Danish.

For one weird moment, all Margit could think of was: "Why me?"

Then a whole series of B-movie plots reeled through her mind, and she pictured herself leaping across the tunnel to the southbound platform and dashing up the escalator to the street above. But she was no athlete like Barbro, and this guy seemed to be in good shape. It wouldn't be easy to outrun the man.

The sudden memory of the knife plunged deep into Søren's back sent a ripple of pure terror through Margit's body. She was standing here talking to a murderer, for God's sake. For a moment she panicked. Sweat rolled down her sides, her hands turned ice cold, and the muscles of her throat clamped around her windpipe so she could hardly breathe.

Then she got mad.

"Who the hell are you, anyway?" she snapped, giving the man at her side a fierce glare.

"That's not important. I just want those runes."

"Well, you're not going to get them," said Margit. And she slammed the heel of her right foot onto the toe of his left shoe, wishing for once that she wore spike heels like Liisa. But the shock of the impact was enough to make the man loosen his grip on her elbow. Margit yanked her arm away, whirled around to her left, and tore down the platform to a bus that was just closing its doors. She slipped inside at the last instant, and stood in the stairwell, panting, as the man with the knife pounded on the side of the bus.

"Don't let him on," Margit pleaded with the bus driver. "Please don't let him on."

"Having a fight with the boyfriend, eh?" said the driver

with a chuckle. "Must be a real humdinger. I saw you stomp on his tootsies. OK, honey, you just go ahead and have a seat." And he put his foot on the gas pedal and pulled swiftly away from the platform, yelling, "Sorry, buddy. Regulations. Can't open the doors once I'm in motion."

Margit sank into an empty seat halfway back in the bus and leaned her flushed face against the cool glass of the window. God, that was close, she thought. That was way too close. Her teeth were chattering and her pulse was racing. She shut her eyes to block out the probing stares of the other passengers and focused all her attention on her breathing.

By the time the bus emerged from the underground tunnel and headed toward Eastlake and the U District, Margit had calmed down enough to open her eyes and stare out at the rain-streaked buildings as they passed. There were two young women sitting behind her, engaged in an earnest conversation, and Margit yielded to the temptation to listen in. She often eavesdropped in restaurants or on buses, and right now she could certainly use some distraction, after what she had just been through. She came in on the middle of a story.

"My mom took care of Mr. Parker for fifteen years," said the woman sitting directly behind Margit. "She loved that man, and every day she'd come home and have some new story to tell about him. Then one day he started to curse her, and she said, 'Mr. Parker, why are you cursing me like that today?' And he said, 'Francine, I'm sorry, I didn't mean to curse you, you know I love you to death.' And my mother knew right away that he was going to die that day, she could tell right off. And when she was ready to leave that afternoon, she said, 'Now don't you go slipping away on me. I want you to be here when I get back tomorrow. Don't you go slipping away overnight.' But the next day he was gone. And my mom was in a precious state when he died. I've never seen her get so upset about a patient before."

The other woman sitting behind Margit clucked in sympathy, and then the first woman finished her story. "And you know," she said, "I miss that Mr. Parker. I never even met him, but I sure do miss him."

Margit blinked back tears, suddenly overcome by a flood of emotions. Sorrow and grief for Søren, mixed with horror at finding him dead; fear, anger, and a great sense of relief that she had escaped the clutches of the man with the knife.

Margit sighed deeply. Stop thinking about all that, she told herself firmly. Relax. And then she reached into her briefcase for the book she had started reading the night before—the latest volume of essays by Klaus Rifbjerg. He was one of the few contemporary authors in Denmark who had a real love for the complexity and nuances of the Danish language, and he was never afraid to stretch the boundaries of conventional prose. Even his nonfiction had an astonishing freshness to it. Margit opened the book to the page where she'd left off, slumped farther down in her seat, and blocked out everything else until the bus reached NE 65th Street.

⌘

At three o'clock Margit finally parked the Mazda in her driveway and turned off the engine. What a day, she thought to herself, as she climbed out of the car and bent down to pet Gregor, who was vigorously rubbing his cheek against the rear bumper. She looked up the street and noted with satisfaction that a shiny black sedan was parked a few houses away. "My bodyguard," she whispered, but she stopped herself from giving a wave.

Her house had been placed under police surveillance.

When Margit got off the bus and walked the short distance to Ralston Automotive, she had already decided that the irritation of Detective Tristano's badgering was nothing compared to the real threat of the man with the knife. That guy meant business, and she didn't want to end up alone with him again. She needed the help of professionals, so she realized that she would have to call the police.

"Hi, Chuck," said Margit as she entered the office of Ralston Automotive, shaking the rain out of her hair. "Boy, it's wet today. Can I use your phone?"

"Sure," said Chuck, glancing up with a smile and then going back to jabbing at the computer keyboard with two fingers. He was looking up some information for a customer who was standing at the counter asking questions about radial tires. Margit was always amazed to find Chuck's computer still in operation, because it was completely covered with a thick layer of grease and grime. She figured it must be an industrial-strength model that could withstand extra abuse.

She got hold of Detective Tristano on the phone, and after a few false starts in the conversation while they traded snide remarks, Margit finally told him about the episode in the bus tunnel.

"I'm sending someone over to watch your house," the detective decided after he heard Margit's account. "The man thinks you've got the runes, so he's bound to show up again sooner or later. Next time he does, we'll take him in. I'm not sure how much of this whole treasure hunt story is true, but if this guy knows something about the murder, then we want him for questioning."

"Knows something about it!" exclaimed Margit impatiently. "Give me a break. He practically said that he did it when he threatened me with his knife."

"OK, Ms. Andersson. Calm down. It was just a manner of speaking. We tend to be a little cautious about accusing people of murder until we've had a chance to talk to them."

Margit tried to interrupt, but the detective cut her off.

"Now don't worry. We wouldn't be sending someone over if we didn't take your story seriously. No matter what, this individual is obviously dangerous, and we're concerned about your safety. Don't do anything foolish, Ms. Andersson. Don't take any long walks alone in the woods, for instance."

"Oh right," said Margit sarcastically. "That's just what I was thinking of doing."

"And if you see anything suspicious, don't hesitate to give us a call," continued Detective Tristano, ignoring her remark. Then he gave her a direct number so she wouldn't have to go through the switchboard.

Margit hung up the phone, her sense of relief outweighing her usual annoyance with the peremptory tone of the detective.

"So how's my old car?" she said, turning to face Chuck, who had finished with the other customer and was now seated on a rickety swivel chair, sipping his coffee from a chipped mug decorated with copulating bunnies.

"All fixed up," said Chuck, setting his cup on the floor and standing up. "Good for at least another five thousand miles. But you're going to need new brakes in a couple of months. They're looking a little worn. If they start getting mushy on you, bring her back in."

"OK," said Margit. "Thanks for doing the tune-up so fast."

"No problem. I always have time for my steady customers," said Chuck with great sincerity. And then he punched a few numbers on the keyboard and pulled her receipt out of the printer.

Margit took her checkbook out of her briefcase and paid the bill. It wasn't cheap, but the work was reliable, and she appreciated Chuck's matter-of-fact approach to car maintenance. He always listened carefully to her description of whatever was ailing her car, and he never sneered at her mention of a slight "ping" in the engine or a whistling noise from the radiator or a scraping sound in the right rear wheel. He didn't expect a non-mechanic to know the correct terminology, and he never felt the need to lecture his customers on the intricate design and complicated functioning of their vehicles. He figured everyone had their own field of expertise, and his happened to be cars—there was no reason to be condescending just because someone didn't know a carburetor from a distributor.

"Thanks again," said Margit as she picked up her car key from the counter. Then she stepped out into the rain to claim the Mazda from the lot in back of the shop.

By the time she reached West Seattle, the rain had stopped and the sun was actually breaking through the clouds. The wind had also dropped off considerably.

As Margit bent down again to pet Gregor's head, she noticed that he was missing his collar. "Oh no," she sighed. "Not again." Every few months he would come home without his collar, blatantly pleased with himself for ditching that annoying accessory.

"Come on in the house," Margit scolded. "You know you can't be out here without an ID tag. What if you get lost?"

Gregor rumbled his protest at such a ridiculous notion but trotted amiably ahead of her up the front path.

Margit unlocked the door, closed it carefully behind her, and set her briefcase on the floor next to the couch. Then she took a new cat collar out of the drawer in the hall table. Good thing she'd bought an extra one last time. It was always such a hassle trying to persuade the pet store owner to put all three names on the tag along with the phone number: Gregor Samsa Andersson. Margit firmly believed that cats deserved the full dignity of a first, middle, and last name. She always felt a little sorry for the elegant white angora that lived across the street. Her tag simply said "Fluffy."

The phone rang as Margit slipped the collar around Gregor's neck and fastened the buckle. He squirmed out of her grasp and sauntered down the hall to the bedroom, ready to curl up on the quilt for his afternoon nap. Margit stood up with a groan, hoping this wasn't going to be one of those days when all the telemarketing companies in the world decided to dial her number. She still had that financial report to translate by tomorrow, and she didn't need any more distractions.

"Hey, Margit!" Renny's cheerful voice exclaimed. "I've been holed up for three days, painting like crazy, but now I could use some company. How about dinner? And it's my treat—I can afford it, since you got me the big grant."

"Oh hi, Renny," said Margit, glad to hear it was her friend

and not some salesman pitching life insurance. "I'd love to, but Liisa gave me an impossible job this morning and it's due by eleven tomorrow. I don't think I have time."

"Sure you do," Renny insisted. "You still have to eat. And how come you're still letting that boss of yours walk all over you? I thought you went freelance so you could set your own schedule. Call her back and tell her the impossible always takes a little longer."

Margit laughed. She did a quick estimate in her head: if she started on the job right now, she could put in a good three hours before dinner. If she was back by ten, she could work until midnight, get six hours sleep, and still have four hours to finish the translation in the morning before she had to deliver it to the agency. It would be tight, but she'd done it before; and she was a pro, after all.

"OK," she told Renny, "You talked me into it. Is 6:30 all right?"

"Perfect. I'll pick you up. I've got a craving for fish, so I'm taking you to that restaurant at Fishermen's Terminal. You still eat fish, don't you?"

"Sure," said Margit. "That sounds great. By the way, did you get the message I left on your machine last night?"

"Uh-huh. I called Preston to see what he could find out for you. He's supposed to call me back this afternoon."

"Do you think he'll be able to track down the guy's name?" asked Margit. She was hoping that Renny's lover might be able to trace the collector who had bought the gold pagoda at Sotheby's.

"He wasn't a hundred percent sure, but he said he'd pull

some strings. Preston has a lot of connections in the art world. If anybody can dig up the name of your collector, he can."

Then Margit promised to be ready at 6:30 and hung up the phone. She took the folder with the Danish job out of her briefcase and slipped it under her arm. She had missed lunch, and all she had for breakfast was a cup of coffee and two pieces of toast, so she was starving.

Margit went into the kitchen, poured herself a large glass of apple juice, and picked up a box of crackers. That would have to hold her until dinner. Then she went down the hall to her study and turned on the computer, which was now back in its normal position on the desk. She put a CD in the player, and for a few minutes she stood and listened to Bonnie Raitt wailing out "No Way to Treat a Lady." Then she sat down to work on that damn financial translation.

13

When Margit and Renny arrived at Chinook's Restaurant at Fishermen's Terminal, the hostess told them it would be at least a twenty-minute wait. She offered them a table in the smoking section that was available right away, but Renny firmly refused.

"No thanks, we'd rather wait. We'll just go out and take a little walk. Can you put us down for a table by the window?"

"Sure," said the young woman, "no problem. Let me give you a beeper, so we can buzz you when your table is ready." And she handed the small black beeper to Renny, who clipped it to the pocket of her jacket.

"Wow," said Margit as they went out the door and turned left toward the passageway leading to the docks. "That's what I call high-class service."

"Yeah," said Renny with a laugh, "I feel just like a doctor or a stockbroker or something. Maybe even a dope dealer, waiting for those urgent calls." She gave the beeper a friendly pat.

It was a chilly evening with a brisk breeze, and Margit pulled on her wool gloves as they walked out to the harbor. The afternoon rain had cleared the air and the stars were out, with only a few thin clouds skimming across the huge yellow orb of the full moon.

"This is great," said Margit with a sigh. "I've been wrestling with stupid accounting terms all afternoon. I really needed to get out in the fresh air."

"Me too," said Renny, buttoning up her jacket. "I've been breathing paint fumes for three days straight, and I was starting to get a little wacky."

On the drive over to the restaurant, Margit had told Renny the whole story about the man with the knife—about her run-in with him at the parking garage, about his attack on Barbro at the museum, and about his attempt to get the runes from her in the bus tunnel earlier in the day. Margit also told her about calling Detective Tristano and getting the police to watch her house.

Renny was suitably outraged by the latest turn of events, and she tried to persuade Margit to come and stay with her.

"You shouldn't be all alone in that house," insisted Renny. "I've got plenty of room in my studio. Why don't you move in with me for a few days?"

"Thanks," said Margit, "but I need to keep working or I won't be able to pay the bills this month, and it would be impossible to move all my equipment over to your place. Besides, I'm not going to let this guy chase me out of my own home. He's caused enough disruption in my life already."

Now, strolling along the docks in the cool, crisp air under the starry sky, neither one of them wanted to give any more thought to knife-wielding burglars or stolen artifacts. It was too nice a night for that.

They walked over to the column that had been erected to

commemorate all those who had lost their lives at sea. A wide bronze band around the base was decorated with a swarm of fish and sea creatures. Renny put out her hand to trace the writhing tentacles of an octopus. On top of the column there was a sculpture of a hearty-looking fisherman lifting his face to the wind as he held onto an enormous halibut he had pulled from the waters. Someone had placed a jar of yellow tulips at the base of the statue, and Margit bent down to look at the accompanying note. "To Knud L. Nordby of the *Northern Star*. May peace be with you," she read.

"Looks like 1980 to '89 was a bad decade," said Renny, peering at the plaques engraved with the names of fishermen lost at sea. "Must be well over a hundred of them."

Margit went over to stand next to her friend, squinting her eyes to read the inscriptions in the dim light. "Lots of Scandinavian names," she said. "Some women, too."

She couldn't help thinking that Søren would probably have preferred to see his name listed here among the missing instead of plastered on the front page of the newspaper. He was a fisherman, after all, and death at sea was always a possibility. And it would certainly have been a more dignified end than expiring in the middle of his living-room floor with a knife in his back.

Then Renny and Margit walked along the water, staring out at the myriad fishing boats rocking gently on their moorings. They made it as far as Dock 8 before a sharp buzz from the beeper called them back to the restaurant.

"I think I'll have the alder-planked halibut and a glass of the Hogue fumé blanc," Renny told the eager young man who had introduced himself as their waiter.

"Excellent choice," he pronounced with a smile. "And for you, ma'am?"

"The Alaskan salmon," said Margit, "Oven broiled. And a bottle of mineral water, please. Talking Rain, if you have it."

"Certainly," said the waiter, writing up their order with a flourish and then dashing off toward the kitchen.

"Not in the mood for wine?" asked Renny.

"No, I've got to go back to work. Wine would just put me to sleep," said Margit, settling more comfortably in her chair.

There was a steady hum of subdued conversation from the nearby tables, pierced once or twice by a delighted squeal from a baby sitting in a highchair at the other end of the restaurant. It was a family place, and crowded even on a Monday night. Margit glanced briefly out the window at the shadowy harbor, where a few tall streetlamps along each dock cast pallid patches of light over the boats.

"Did Preston get back to you this afternoon?" asked Margit.

"Oh God, yes," exclaimed Renny. "I forgot all about it. Your story about the museum and the bus tunnel knocked it right out of my mind. It seems so odd that the guy with the knife is really a wealthy collector. Somehow I can't quite connect the two. But wait till you hear this—Preston found out some stuff that you won't even believe.

"He called up a few of his colleagues and got them to snoop around for him. Collectors are a secretive bunch, and it wasn't easy to track this guy down. Preston really had to dig to find out anything, but he ended up getting quite an earful. He told me that nobody would confirm it for sure, but rumor has it that the gold coin auctioned off at Sotheby's was sold to a certain Carsten Næslund, a Danish collector who inherited a nice little fortune from his father back in 1985."

"Two years before the pagoda was sold," mused Margit.

"Uh-huh," said Renny. "It seems that the senior Mr. Næslund was a respected curator at the National Museum in Copenhagen—and you wouldn't think that type of job would bring in large sums of money. But apparently he was a shrewd investor, and he put all his savings into a few lucky ventures that really paid off. He helped finance the Swedish designer who invented the milk carton that we use today, and he was one of Bjørn Wiinblad's early patrons. He also bought quite a few shares in Bang & Olufsen when they first started out, and he was even among the original backers of the pop group ABBA."

"You're kidding," said Margit, hearing in her mind the insipid harmonies of that Swedish foursome. She had never been able to understand their popularity.

"Nope, I'm not kidding," said Renny. "The man apparently had a real knack for knowing what would make money. Anyway, Mr. Næslund hoarded his riches and continued in his job at the museum, the same as always, until he retired in 1980. Few people knew about his wealth, and he never shared any of it with his son. In fact, the story goes that he even threatened to cut Carsten out of his will. But apparently the old man relented before he died, and the son inherited the whole pot of gold, so to speak."

"Why would he want to disinherit his son?" asked Margit.

"That's the interesting part of the story. It turns out that Carsten was actually following in his father's footsteps, and he earned himself a degree in archaeology from the University of

Uppsala. He became quite an expert on the Viking Age, and he wrote some influential treatises on his work in the field. But eventually something went wrong with Carsten, and he wound up being ousted from the profession. His colleagues even gave him a derogatory nickname."

"What was that?" asked Margit.

"The Rogue Archaeologist," said Renny with a grin. "It seems there were strong suspicions that Carsten had slipped a few artifacts into his pocket and walked off a dig with them. Just small things that he thought no one would miss—like a silver Thor's hammer and a gold fibula."

"You mean a gold leg bone?" interrupted Margit, looking puzzled.

"No," laughed Renny. "A fibula is a brooch with a safety-pin type of clasp. It was common in Roman times, and I guess the trade with the Romans brought the fashion north. I remember seeing pictures of fibulas in a class I once took called 'Art of the Ancient World.'

"Anyway," she continued, "Carsten apparently decided to swipe two of these priceless and irreplaceable relics. He denied all charges, and nothing was ever proved, but the items never turned up again. And nobody wanted to hire him after that. They didn't want to risk having someone on the site who had an uncontrollable lust for treasures—no matter how much of an expert he was."

"So what did he do then?"

"According to Preston's source, Carsten got himself hooked up with a group of collectors who were interested in buying ancient artifacts as tax write-offs—mostly Americans. He would evaluate the object that was up for sale and tell them whether it was a good investment or not. The trick was to buy a valuable item and then donate it to a museum and get a tax write-off for two or three times the purchase price thanks to Carsten's inflated appraisal. He made himself a good living as a consultant until somebody blew the whistle on the scam, and he was out of a job again."

"And I don't suppose his father was interested in supporting him," said Margit.

"No way," replied Renny. "Apparently Carsten was a bad apple right from the start, but his father didn't want to admit it openly. When Carsten was a kid, he had free run of the National Museum, and he just couldn't keep his hands off all the Viking stuff. There were rumors of some hushed-up incidents of theft — items that were removed from exhibits for cleaning or research and then mysteriously disappeared."

The museum had been one of Margit's favorite haunts back when she was a grad student living in Copenhagen. She had vivid memories of wandering through the endless rooms lined with display cases containing thousands of small gold objects recovered from grave sites or pulled out of the Danish bogs. Most of them weren't even labeled. She could easily imagine a young kid looking at all those treasures and deciding that one small piece surely wouldn't be missed. She wondered how things looked now, after the recent renovation at the museum.

"Huh," said Margit. "Why is it that Carsten is starting to remind me of our other thief — Niels Heidenreich?"

"I know what you mean," said Renny. "I've got that feeling too. Anyway, when the father died, Carsten decided to use his inheritance to become a collector himself. Preston says that he managed to acquire some real treasures over the years, and among collectors he's known for his ruthless drive to get what he wants. And they say he's not a good sport about losing."

"I bet," said Margit, remembering the malice in the man's eyes when she refused to hand over the runes.

At that moment the waiter appeared at their table and solicitously placed two piping hot plates of food in front of them. Renny and Margit immediately put Carsten Næslund out of their minds and turned all their attention to their dinner. They were both famished.

⌘

Forty minutes later, Margit put down her decaf cappuccino and leaned back lazily in her chair, glad that she hadn't allowed herself to be tempted by that fresh Peach Slump for dessert. Don't do it, she told herself sternly, as Renny ordered mint tea and a thick wedge of cheesecake.

"Sure you don't want anything?" her friend asked again.

Margit stubbornly shook her head. "I'll pass," she said. "Just coffee for me."

"Well, I'm celebrating," said Renny. "Getting that grant was a real godsend. I already told Bob that I need to cut back my hours at the café. He wasn't happy about it, but he knows I've got to paint, so we agreed on twenty-five hours a week, starting on Friday. I'm going to be painting up a storm, thanks to you, kiddo." And she raised her glass in a toast and then finished off the last of her wine.

After devouring her dessert and paying the bill, Renny got up to find the restroom. "Too much tea," she said. "It goes right through me. Back in a sec," and she left Margit to finish her coffee alone.

The restaurant had almost cleared out, and the only diners close enough to observe were an elderly man and woman eating their meal in stolid silence.

Been married too long, thought Margit, staring at the woman who was chewing her food with an air of resignation, her eyes fixed on her plate. The husband slopped another huge spoonful of sour cream onto his baked potato. Then he picked up his fork and lifted a dripping chunk of halibut to his lips, shoving the fish into his cavernous mouth. He never once looked at his wife.

Used up all their conversation years ago, concluded Margit. Now they're just bored with each other. That couldn't happen to us, she thought, remembering the last time she and Joe had eaten out together in Santa Fe. Was it really only ten days ago?

They were sitting in a little café on the Plaza—nothing fancy about the place, but the food was always excellent, and they had eaten there many times before. Joe ordered the chile relleno, and Margit asked for a cheese enchilada. They were both drinking wine and talking about a Woody Allen movie, laughing at the scene where a painter pompously explains his theory that an artist can create his own moral universe.

Margit looked into Joe's warm brown eyes flecked with amber and reached across the table to put her hand in his. He lifted her hand to his lips and then began languidly sucking on her fingers, one after the other, keeping his eyes on her face. Margit felt a shiver of pleasure race down her spine. Then Joe laughed softly and started telling her about the Henry Moore biography he had been reading.

Margit loved this man. She couldn't get enough of Joe's tender touch, his deep voice, or his familiar grin. And they always had so much to talk about.

Two glasses clinked together as a busboy cleared off the table behind Margit. She blinked her eyes, surprised to find herself still staring at the elderly couple mechanically eating their dinner. Their lethargy and remoteness chilled her to the bone.

"Please don't let that happen to us," she murmured fervently.

Then Margit deliberately turned away and focused her gaze on the wooden panel along the window. It was painted bright red and decorated with old labels from cans of salmon: Northern Pride, Sea Chef, Snowcap, Harp, Coleman Flag, Humes Karluk. Margit scanned each label briefly and then picked up the blue container of Baleine sea salt crystals from the table. She was idly pouring a little mound of salt into the palm of her hand when a sudden flash of light outdoors caught her eye. She glanced out the window and then jumped up so abruptly that her chair keeled over and crashed to the floor.

The elderly couple flinched and for a split second they stared into each other's astounded eyes, but then they shifted their glance and returned to methodically chewing their food.

"My God!" exclaimed Margit. "That's it!"

"What's going on?" demanded Renny, rushing up to the table. "What's wrong?"

Margit lowered her voice. "Look out there," she said, pointing to the window. "See that boat pulling away from the dock? Look at the name on the back."

"So?" Renny leaned up close to the window and put her hands around her face to block out the light from the restaurant. "What about it?"

"It's part of Søren's message," Margit said urgently. "Don't you remember?"

"No, I don't get it." Renny stepped back from the window and gave her friend a quizzical look.

"The first line of runes," prompted Margit. "'My name is WigoR, the knower of dangerous things.' It's not a person, like I thought. It's not even a Danish name. Didn't you see what it said on that boat?"

Renny turned back to the window, staring at the tiny lights of the vessel fast disappearing into the night.

Margit leaned closer and whispered, "The name of that boat is the *Vigor*."

14

At six a.m. the shrill scream of the alarm clock rousted Margit out of a deep sleep. "Not yet," she groaned, rolling over to the edge of the bed to jab at the off button.

She had stayed up too late, wrangling with a particularly opaque section of the Danish financial report. By one o'clock Margit realized that fatigue was making her sloppy, and she would have to get some sleep before she could finish the job. She stripped off her clothes, pulled on an old flannel nightgown, and fell into bed. She slept like a rock, without a single nightmare to disturb her dreams.

Ten more minutes, Margit promised herself, you can have ten more minutes before you have to get up.

The next time she opened her eyes to glance at the clock, the red digits warned that it was already 6:35, and she threw off the covers with a grunt of dismay. Only three and a half hours to finish that translation. She'd better get moving.

Margit put on her bathrobe and trudged out to the kitchen to switch on the coffeemaker. Then she let Gregor out the front door, taking note of the black sedan now parked directly across the street. "Morning, boys," she murmured, glad to know that other people had to get up even earlier than she did to start their work day. Or maybe they'd been there all night.

Then she went into the bathroom to brush her teeth. The glare of the fluorescent light was too much for her, and she snapped it off again. She picked up the toothpaste in the dim glow of the nightlight, peering at her scraggly hair and bleary features in the mirror. "You're looking good, girl," Margit muttered to herself. "Sure looking good today." Then she stuck the toothbrush in her mouth.

The next instant she was leaning over the sink, retching and spitting, trying to rid her tongue and palate of the cloying slime of Gregor's Petromalt. The tube of oily hairball medicine was red and white, just like the toothpaste tube, and she must have left it on the sink last night after she found Gregor throwing up on the bathroom floor. At the time she was grateful he had decided not to do it on the living-room rug again. Now she wished that he had.

Margit rinsed her mouth thoroughly with peppermint Scope and then headed for the kitchen and a strong cup of coffee. Ten minutes later she switched on her computer, put on Tina Turner's *Simply the Best*, and then sat down in her robe to finish that financial report.

⌘

By eleven o'clock, Margit was driving along Elliott Avenue, heading back toward Fishermen's Terminal. She had delivered the completed translation with time to spare, and for once there were no more jobs waiting for her, so she didn't have to argue with Liisa about taking the afternoon off.

A long hot shower and a good breakfast had restored her sense of humor, and she had even been able to joke with Lars about her new brand of toothpaste when she ran into him at the agency. But she didn't mention her discovery from the night before.

After the fishing boat had vanished from view, Renny had turned away from the restaurant window and promptly said, "Let's go call the cops."

But Margit resisted. "There's nothing they can do tonight, and who knows where that boat is headed. I'll call them tomorrow."

Renny got suspicious. "You're not thinking of doing anything stupid, are you Margit? A little investigating of your own, or something? Remember who you're dealing with here. That Carsten Næslund is not a nice guy."

"Don't worry," Margit had assured her friend. "I'll call the police tomorrow." And she fully intended to keep her promise, but not until she had a chance to talk to the owner of that boat herself. Carsten obviously didn't know what clues the runes contained, so she had a head start on tracking down the treasure. And she was suddenly seized with a giddy sense of excitement at the prospect of actually finding the fourth Golden Horn.

Now Margit was heading for Magnolia, steering the Mazda confidently across the high span of the bridge above Terminal 91. It was a bright sunny day, and she was in a good mood.

She glanced out the window to her right, sweeping her eyes

over the colorful ranks of new cars, just off the boat from Japan and awaiting delivery. She sincerely hoped that Chuck could keep her old car running for a few more years. Margit cringed at the thought of facing the smarmy and aggressive familiarity of those new-car salesmen, who were always too anxious to close a deal. For political reasons she had already decided to buy an American model next time, but she hadn't yet driven one that she liked. And she wasn't prepared for the shock of monthly car payments.

Margit reached the end of the bridge and then headed along the bluff. She was determined to take a roundabout route to her destination, just in case Carsten was trying to tail her, although she hadn't noticed any dark-blue Volvos on the road. She figured he was smart enough to realize that the police were watching her house by now, but he might have staked out the agency and followed her from Belltown. There was no harm in taking precautions, at any rate, and it would be easy to lose him in the maze of Magnolia streets.

When Margit reached Fishermen's Terminal, she parked her car in the lot near the bank and walked slowly toward the harbor, wondering how best to introduce herself to the owner of the *Vigor*. By the time she had passed the laundromat reserved for commercial fishermen and the commemorative column on the wharf, she had decided that the truth was really her only option.

Margit strolled along Dock 4, trying to look casual as she searched for the *Vigor* among the motley collection of fishing boats lined up along the pier. She passed the *Sarah Rose*, the *Sea Rover*, and the *Clementina*. She noticed the "For Sale" signs taped crookedly to the wheelhouse windows of three or four boats, giving them a melancholy air. And she laughed at a bumper sticker plastered on the bow of a decrepit-looking vessel: "Jesus was a gillnetter."

Close to the end of the dock, Margit finally came upon the *Vigor*, rocking gently in its berth. It was a small, scruffy boat with two long poles sticking straight up midship. She was unsure about the proper etiquette for summoning the skipper of a fishing vessel, and she didn't want to step aboard without permission, so she resorted to shouting: "Hello—anybody home?"

A grizzled old man with impish brown eyes and thick white hair stuck his head out the wheelhouse door. "You talking to me?" he asked. "Are you talking to *me?*" And then he chuckled at his own imitation of DeNiro in that scene from *Taxi Driver*.

"Uh, yes. Yes, I am. Good morning," said Margit, stumbling a bit over her words. This encounter wasn't starting off exactly as she had expected. "My name is Margit Andersson, and I wonder if I could talk to you for a few minutes. It's about Søren Rasmussen."

"Ahh," said the fisherman, "poor old Søren." The smile disappeared from his face, and he shook his head somberly, making a little clucking noise with his tongue. "You a cop?" he asked suddenly, eyeing Margit with suspicion.

"No, I was his friend," she said staunchly.

"Good. Don't much care for cops. All right, then. Why don't you come in and sit down. I was just fixing myself a snack. Maybe you'd like to join me. Morris Talbot's the name, by the way. Here, let me give you a hand." And he helped Margit step on board.

The cramped quarters of the wheelhouse were obviously both home and workplace for the old man, and the jumble of fishing gear, worn clothing, and miscellaneous household items reminded Margit of Søren's cluttered house. It took her a moment to get used to the slight rolling motion of the boat, and she was glad that she wasn't susceptible to seasickness, the way Renny was. But the smell of fish nearly overpowered her.

"Here, have a seat," said Morris, picking up a pile of newspapers from a low stool and stuffing them under the narrow unmade bed. "Wasn't expecting company," he added with a grin.

"I'm sorry to bother you," began Margit, but Morris waved her apologies aside.

"Don't get me wrong. It's not every day that a man my age gets a visit from a pretty young lady. Can't say as it's happened even once in the past few years. Nope, don't recall that it has, and my memory's still sharp. Nothing wrong with the old brain cells, even though I'm over ninety."

"You're ninety years old?" asked Margit, unable to hide her disbelief.

"Ninety-one next month," said Morris with satisfaction. "Planning to stick around for the millennium, too. Wouldn't want to miss the party. Now, how about that snack?" And he started pulling provisions out of a small built-in cupboard.

Margit accepted a piece of rye bread with a hunk of caraway cheese, but she declined the sardines in tomato sauce and the shot of Southern Comfort.

"Keeps the old joints greased," said Morris, tossing back his drink and pouring himself another. He was sitting on the rumpled bed with a plate of food on his lap and the bottle of liquor at his feet. "So you said you wanted to talk to me about Søren?"

"Yes," said Margit. She looked into the intense brown eyes

of the old man, and decided she would have to trust him with the whole story. If Morris—or his boat—was the "knower of dangerous things," then he was not going to reveal any secrets unless she convinced him that Søren would want her to know. "It's kind of a long story," she said, and then she told him about finding Søren murdered, about the runes and the pictures from the Golden Horns, about the attempted burglaries and the man with the knife. She told him everything that had happened so far, right up to spotting the name on his boat as he pulled out of the harbor the night before.

Morris listened attentively as he munched on his bread and sardines, occasionally bending down to pour himself some more Southern Comfort. By the time Margit had finished her account, the bottle was half empty, but the liquor didn't seem to be having any ill effects on the old man. If anything, he seemed more alert than ever.

"That's one helluva story, young lady," Morris finally said. "Just about the darndest thing I ever heard. I've known Søren for a long time, and he was always a little peculiar, but I had no idea he was mixed up in something like this." He shook his head in bewilderment.

"You didn't?" said Margit, feeling disappointment sweep over her. "You mean Søren never told you anything about any of this? Nothing at all?"

"Nope. Can't say as he did. He was real close-mouthed about his personal affairs, you know. I met him back in '77. Ran into him at the Valhalla and we got to talking. His English wasn't all that great. He'd only been in this country a couple of years. But we hit it off, and I ended up hiring him to teach me about fishing."

Morris got up to put his plate in a plastic basin that already held a stack of dirty dishes. He took Margit's plate from her, added it to the pile, and then returned to his seat on the bed.

"I'm not a real fisherman, you know," he confessed with a grin. "Not like Søren or the other old-timers around here—not by a long shot. Spent my whole life working for the railroad, as a matter of fact. The Northern Pacific, going back and forth between Seattle and Chicago. Retired in '75 and spent the next two years wondering what the hell to do with myself. My wife died a long time ago and my kids had their own families to take care of. Then one day I was sitting in my easy chair, watching a rerun of 'Petticoat Junction,' and I said to myself, 'Morris, old boy, you're not doing yourself a darn bit of good sitting here and listening to this drivel.' And I decided right then and there to buy myself a boat."

Morris chuckled. Margit smiled politely, but she was starting to feel rather gloomy, wondering whether she was ever going to make any sense out of Søren's obscure message—why on earth did he have to be so cagey?

"The one thing I missed about the railroad," Morris continued, "was being on the move. I never liked staying in one place too long, and retirement was driving me nuts. So I thought to myself: why not get a fishing boat and kill two birds with one stone? I could make a little extra cash and keep myself out of the loony bin or the old folks home at the same time. So I bought this boat and named it the *Vigor*, as a reminder that life isn't over till it's over."

Morris laughed heartily and lifted his glass toward Margit in a toast.

"And then you hired Søren to teach you about fishing?" prompted Margit, trying to bring the old man back to the original topic, even though she had lost all hope that Morris knew anything that would help solve the puzzle.

"That's right. He taught me everything I know about trolling. We spent a lot of time together when he was teaching me the ropes. Used to go out salmon fishing in the Sound. He didn't have a real boat of his own, just a small skiff, so he seemed glad to hook up with me—though he never actually came out and said so. Sometimes I'd let him take the *Vigor* out alone, and I could tell he liked that a lot. But I haven't seen him much in the past few years. Can't say we were really pals, either. Søren was too much of a loner for that, and he liked people to mind their own business."

"When did you last see him?" asked Margit.

"Must be at least six months ago," said Morris, stroking his chin. "That's right, I remember now. It was last September— the day after one of my buddies came back from halibut fishing in Alaska, and we'd been out celebrating the night before. I was feeling a little under the weather, you might say, when Søren showed up and asked me if he could stow some gear on board."

"What kind of gear?" asked Margit, her eyes widening and her heart giving a jump.

"Looked like a bunch of old clothes and a coil of rope, near as I could tell," said Morris. "He often kept stuff on board, back when we were doing a lot of fishing together. I didn't mind, because he tucked it all away in a little cupboard that he kept locked up."

"Locked up?" repeated Margit, hardly daring to hope.

"Uh-huh. Told me he didn't mean any offense but he didn't trust most folks and he'd just as soon not tempt anybody. So he got himself a fancy padlock."

"Did you clear out Søren's stuff after you heard about the murder? Did you tell the police about it?" Margit asked, trying not to sound too anxious.

"Nope," said Morris, shaking his head. "Been thinking about it, but haven't gotten around to it yet. Didn't think it would really interest the police or anybody else. Søren was just the paranoid type—he didn't have anything worth stealing." But as he uttered these words, Morris suddenly realized that he might have been greatly mistaken, and the full significance of Margit's story finally hit him.

"You don't really think..." said Morris.

The next minute he was down on his knees, sliding out a tool chest from under the bed. He tossed out a couple of wrenches, a hammer, and a large screwdriver.

"What are you doing?" asked Margit, caught off guard by his sudden frenzy.

"Looking for something to break open the lock with," Morris told her. "It's a good solid lock and I don't know the combination."

"But *I* do," said Margit. "I'm almost positive I know what it is."

15

M orris Talbot sat back on his heels and gave Margit an astonished look. "What do you mean?" he asked. "How come you know the combination?"

"The second line of runes that Søren sent me," said Margit, her face flushed with excitement. "The three numbers in the right place. I'll bet you a million bucks those numbers are the combination to Søren's lock."

"I'm not a betting man," said Morris with a grin, "especially when the odds are against me."

He stood up and moved over to the right side of the wheel-house. He picked up a pair of old rubber boots, a stack of tattered *Life* magazines, and a broken toaster oven, and dumped them all onto the deck a few feet away. Then he tugged at a heavy cardboard box filled with cans of string beans, pulling it back from the wall and shoving it aside.

"It's over here," he said, squatting down in front of a small cupboard door about two feet square.

Margit got up and went over to Morris. She knelt down beside him and stared at the heavy-duty padlock with its thick hoop of metal and shiny black dial. It looked brand-new. She took a deep breath and then put her right hand up to the calibrated knob. It was cold to her touch, and she noticed that her fingers were trembling.

Margit spun the dial clockwise, one full turn, and then stopped precisely on 22. She eased it to the left until 15 was straight up, then she turned it right again to the number 4. She gave the lock a good yank. Nothing happened.

"You've gotta go past zero," urged Morris, pressing his face closer to the lock. "Let me try." And he deftly spun the dial, taking it through its paces in two seconds flat. There was a little click as he reached the number 4. Then he pulled the padlock smoothly apart, lifted it out of the sturdy latch, and opened the cupboard door.

Margit leaned down and peered into the dark, musty cubbyhole. She reached inside and dragged out a pile of old clothes, a coil of rope, and a rusty crowbar.

There was nothing else in the cupboard.

"Give me a flashlight," commanded Margit, refusing to accept the obvious. She could have screamed in disappointment.

Morris handed her a big rubber-coated flashlight, and they both stared into the illuminated space, which was quite empty.

"I feel just like Geraldo, cracking open Al Capone's safe on prime-time TV," said Morris with a sigh. "There wasn't a darn thing in it except for a couple of old whiskey bottles or something. What a joke." And he went back to his seat on the bed and poured himself a double shot of Southern Comfort.

Margit sat on the floor next to Søren's old clothes, muttering to herself and crumpling the faded fabric in an angry fist. "Goddamn you, Søren Rasmussen," she sputtered, lifting a pair of dusty coveralls in the air and throwing them with all her might against the side of the wheelhouse. "How could you do this to me? How could you?" By now she was shouting.

"Here," said Morris, handing Margit the bottle of liquor with a look of concern on his face. "Have a slug of this. I think you need it."

Margit took a long swallow, grateful for the fiery warmth coursing down her throat. She leaned back against the bulkhead, clutching the bottle of Southern Comfort in her right hand, and wearily closed her eyes.

The worn coveralls had slithered down the opposite wall and landed in a heap on the deck. There was something sticking out of the front pocket.

"Hey, what's that?" said Morris, pointing to a yellowish-white strip that was visible above the drab green edge of the pocket.

"I don't know and I don't care," said Margit, barely opening her eyes to see what he was talking about. She had had enough of Søren and his whole ridiculous treasure hunt.

But Morris was curious. He went over and pulled a folded piece of yellowed paper out of the pocket of the coveralls.

"Huh," he grunted, "what do you make of this?" And he handed the paper to Margit, who put down the liquor bottle and couldn't resist running her eyes over the page.

It was a badly spotted copy of an old vehicle registration form for a 1970 VW bug, issued to one Wilhelmina Rasmussen. When Margit noticed the familiar address on NW 58th Street, she realized she was holding a document that had once belonged to Søren's sister-in-law—his brother Ole's wife. The form had expired in '75, the same year Søren inherited his brother's house and moved to the States. The license number was XX6263, and there was a heavy black circle drawn around it.

"Mean anything to you?" asked Morris, sitting down on the bed again.

"No, it doesn't," said Margit peevishly. "And I sure am sick of all these paranoid games. Why couldn't Søren just put the Golden Horn in the cupboard, like any normal person would have done? We finally solve all his riddles, and now he's still leading us on a wild-goose chase. It's not fair."

Margit got to her feet, folded up the piece of paper, and impatiently stuck it in her jacket pocket. She dusted off her jeans and ran her hand through her hair.

"Maybe he just had the horn melted down and stashed the dough in some Swiss bank account that no one will ever find," she said in disgust, although she sincerely doubted that Søren would have destroyed a national treasure for the sake of money—no matter how princely the sum. It just didn't fit with what she knew about him.

"What are you going to do now?" asked Morris.

"I'm going to tell Detective Tristano about this piece of paper and then go back home and take a nice hot bath. Let the police go chasing around town. I've had enough of this whole business."

Then Margit sighed and held out her hand to Morris. "Well, thanks for all your help. It certainly has been interesting—no doubt about that."

The old fisherman stood up and gave her hand a friendly squeeze. "It's been a pleasure," he said warmly. "Really made my day, even if we didn't find the gold. Come back and visit anytime. Maybe you'd like to go out for a little spin around the Sound?"

"Sure, I'd like that," said Margit, smiling at his rather wistful invitation.

And then Morris ushered her out the wheelhouse door. As Margit walked back along the dock she could still hear him in the distance, whistling a tune that sounded an awful lot like the theme music to "Petticoat Junction."

⌘

There were three blue and white phone booths lined up at the east end of Fishermen's Terminal, but Margit took one look inside and decided to wait to call the detective from her car phone instead. The square fluorescent lights in the ceiling of each booth were literally crawling with big black spiders. The posted sign urging her to "talk as long as you like for one dollar anywhere in Western Washington" was not enough of an enticement to make Margit step into any of those booths.

Detective Tristano's direct line was busy when she tried to reach him from her car, so she called the police department switchboard and left a brief message.

When Margit finally pulled into her driveway, it was almost four o'clock, and she was feeling exhausted. She decided to treat herself to that hot bath she had mentioned to Morris, but first she had a little errand to take care of.

Margit climbed out of the Mazda and strolled up the block, with Gregor eagerly trotting along beside her. She crossed the street and walked up to the driver's side of a shiny white

Chevy parked in front of Bernie Ashwood's house. She leaned down and tapped on the window.

The plainclothes police officer sitting in the front seat had just dozed off for a minute. He'd been on duty for nine hours straight, and his replacement was late.

An irritating clicking noise made him open his eyes, and he suddenly found the subject of his surveillance peering at him from six inches away. The officer rolled down his window with a look of alarm.

"Everything all right, Miss?" he asked.

"Fine and dandy," said Margit. "Here's something for Detective Tristano." And she handed him the expired vehicle registration form through the window. "Tell him I found this in some clothes that Søren Rasmussen left with a friend. Ask him if he can look up the license number and find out what happened to this old VW bug. I think it might be an important lead in the case."

Margit stepped back from the unmarked police car and gave the officer a little wave. "Keep up the good work," she said, and then she and Gregor walked back to their house.

An hour and a half later the phone rang just as Margit was stepping out of the tub. She grabbed a bath towel, thinking that for once she would let the answering machine handle the call. But the deeply ingrained fear of losing out on paying work, which tormented every freelancer, finally got the better of her. She threw the towel around her shoulders and rushed into her study to pick up the phone on the fourth ring.

"Hello?" she said, out of breath.

"Ms. Andersson? Detective Tristano here, reporting back on that important lead you gave us."

Margit was not pleased to hear that he seemed to be chuckling. "Well? What did you find out?"

"Mr. Rasmussen sold his sister-in-law's VW to a used-car dealer back in 1975, a few months after he arrived in the States," said the detective. "The vehicle then passed through a number of owners until it ended up at its present location." He sounded inexplicably gleeful.

"And where's that?" asked Margit, starting to feel chilled. Her hair was dripping in her face, and she was standing in a little puddle of water.

"In the clutches of the Fremont Troll," hooted Detective Tristano, and then the full force of his mirth overtook him.

Margit could hear him coughing and choking on the other end of the line as he tried in vain to suppress his laughter. She held the receiver at arm's length, waiting for him to regain his composure.

"Would you mind telling me what you're talking about?" she finally asked in her frostiest tone of voice.

"Sorry," gasped the detective, clearly mortified at his loss of professional decorum. "My apologies, Ms. Andersson. No offense intended."

Margit rolled her eyes and scowled but refrained from commenting.

"It seems that the last owner of the vehicle decided to donate the car to one of the sculptors who was building the troll under the Aurora bridge," continued the detective. "And that's where it's been since 1990. Embedded in concrete. I don't really see that it's relevant to Mr. Rasmussen's case. Do you?"

"No, I guess not," Margit grudgingly had to agree. She vividly remembered seeing that beat-up orange VW with its rear axle sunk into the ground and the huge fingers of the troll's left hand curled over its hood and roof.

The Fremont Troll was a popular tourist attraction, and Margit herself had taken out-of-town visitors over to see the enormous hulking figure rising up out of the dusty embankment under the north end of the bridge. The troll had thick ropy hair falling over the right side of his face and a long sloping nose. His one visible eye, made from some kind of giant reflector, had an angry glint to it. In the daytime the troll was always swarming with tourists who climbed up behind his giant head to have their pictures taken. At night, the troll and the dark crawlspace under the bridge became a hangout for teenagers, prompting frequent patrols by the police.

Margit realized that it would have been impossible for Søren to hide his treasure anywhere near the troll unobserved. There were just too many people around. And it seemed highly improbable that he would have risked damaging the Golden Horn by somehow managing to conceal it in the car before it was encased in cement.

Maybe it was just a coincidence that the registration form was in the pocket of Søren's old coveralls. He was an inveterate pack rat, after all, and he never threw anything away. But if the document was intended to be a clue in this crazy treasure hunt, then Søren had failed to convey his message clearly enough. They had come to a dead end.

"Why did you think this was so important?" Detective Tristano asked.

Margit hesitated for a moment, but then told him the whole story of her meeting with Morris Talbot aboard the *Vigor*. She decided that she might as well tell him the final solution to the runes, since she'd given up on discovering anything more herself. And the thought of a confrontation between the dapper detective and the tough old fisherman who didn't like cops almost made up for the detective's rude outburst of laughter. Maybe Morris would even do his DeNiro imitation for the police.

Margit hung up the phone before Detective Tristano could give her a lecture on the folly of private citizens snooping around in an official murder investigation. She could tell he didn't like the fact that she had figured out the runes on her own. He was even more disapproving of her decision to open Søren's cupboard without calling in the police. But what was done was done. And it was the detective's case now—she washed her hands of the whole business.

Gregor was circling around at her feet, rubbing his cheek on the legs of her desk, and complaining loudly. He wanted his dinner, and Margit realized suddenly that she was hungry too. The bread and cheese that Morris had served her didn't amount to much of a lunch, and low blood sugar was making her cranky.

"OK, let's have some food," she told Gregor. "Just give me a second to get dressed."

Five minutes later, Margit opened a can of tuna, dished up a generous portion, and put Gregor's plate in its usual spot on the floor next to the stove. He took one sniff at the food, wiggled his tail with disdain, and walked away.

"Hey, come back here and eat your dinner," Margit yelled after him. "You can't have Kitty Stew every night." But Gregor was already halfway to the bedroom. When he got hungry enough, he'd be back.

Margit opened a can of organic tomato soup for herself, and then put together a small salad while she waited for the soup to cook.

She sat down to eat at the dining-room table, sifting through the stack of mail that she'd picked up at her post office box on the way home. The usual bills and ads, nothing much of interest except for an announcement of a big sale at Magnolia Hi-Fi. On the front page Margit noticed a picture of the CD player that Joe had been wanting for his studio, and it was marked 50% off. She decided to buy it for him as an early birthday present. If she left soon, she could make it out to the store and still get back in time to watch "Frasier" on the tube.

It was one of the few TV shows that Margit watched regularly, even though she was always griping to Renny about the mistakes in the script. The Seattle setting was obviously only a token gesture. Local residents laughed at the references to squeegee guys washing car windshields, and streets with names like "Cherokee Avenue"—none of which had a scrap of geographic authenticity. She figured the show's writers must all be from New York.

Margit quickly finished her dinner, put the dishes in the sink, and went into the bedroom to say goodbye to Gregor before she left. He was curled up in a ball on the quilt, but he opened his eyes and blinked at her when she petted his bulky head.

Then Margit put on her jean jacket, picked up her shoulder bag, and went out the front door.

Heavy clouds had moved in, covering the stars and blocking out any moonlight. It smelled like rain. The forecasters were predicting overcast skies and colder temperatures for the rest of the week. Margit shivered as she sat in the driver's seat, rubbing her hands together as she waited for the engine to warm up.

The white Chevy down the block had been replaced by another of the anonymous black sedans. Margit gave the cops a little smile of acknowledgment, glad that she had decided to let the professionals handle the case from now on. She didn't even care about not finding the Golden Horn. She simply didn't want to think about it anymore.

She hoped the police would track down Carsten soon and haul him in for questioning so she could stop looking over her shoulder. She hoped they would find enough evidence to convict him of murdering Søren. That's all that really mattered. Maybe someday the ancient relic would turn up. Maybe it would never be found. Margit just wanted to put the whole thing out of her mind.

For once she didn't have any rush translation jobs hanging over her head, and she was stubbornly determined not to let anything—not even thieves or gold artifacts—interfere with her free evening. She was going out to buy a birthday present for her lover. Then she would come home, watch TV, and go to bed early—like any other normal person on a normal weeknight.

Margit turned on her headlights, backed out of the driveway, and headed for the West Seattle bridge, listening to Clapton's "No Alibis" as she drove.

But for the second time in as many weeks, she should have had some premonition that things were about to go wrong.

16

F rom the West Seattle bridge, Margit took the turnoff for the
viaduct, deciding that Aurora Avenue would be a better
route to choose than the freeway, especially since it had started
to rain. People always drove too close in the rain, as if they were
trying to huddle their cars together to stay dry. This inevitably
led to multiple rear-enders, and at 60 miles an hour that could
mean some serious accidents. So Margit opted for the somewhat
slower and less traveled road.

There was a surprising amount of traffic for a Tuesday
night, even on the viaduct. Must be something going on at the
Kingdome, thought Margit, as she let a young hotshot roar past
her in his low-rider truck. Then she moved into the far left lane
and glanced out over the harbor, lined with huge orange cranes
that always reminded her of giant giraffes. In the bright arc
lights an enormous container ship with a Korean flag fluttering
from its stern loomed up next to the dock, waiting to be un-
loaded.

In the distance Margit could see the outline of a ferryboat
slowly plowing its way through the choppy water toward

Bainbridge Island. The boat's lights were strung along its side like phosphorescent beads.

The lumbering shape of a 747 hovered overhead, red warning lights blinking, and she wondered where all those passengers were going. She had a friend who worked for the airlines and knew all the local flight schedules by heart. In the daytime, he could look up at a passing jet, take note of the logo on the tail, check his watch, and then tell her exactly where the plane was headed or where it was coming in from.

Margit passed the Coast Guard cutters and the old Alaska boat terminal. "Pier 48," it said on the illuminated façade, "Port of Seattle." She passed the ferry terminal to Winslow and Bremerton. She noted the long line of piers with old warehouses that had been renovated and filled with restaurants and souvenir shops. Pier 56, Pier 57, Pier 58.

She glanced at the deserted wet planks of Pier 62/63, thinking how incredibly small it looked. Every summer the bare pier was reincarnated as the site for a series of outdoor rock concerts. The sudden mushrooming of a carnival-like set on the normally empty pier made it seem ten times its size. Margit had taken Joe to see Lyle Lovett the year before, only a few months after they first met. The memory of sitting outside in the mild summer evening, staring at the brightly lit stage against the dark backdrop of Elliott Bay and listening to Lyle's zany lyrics, would be forever linked in her mind with the surging euphoria of falling in love.

Margit shifted her gaze back to the road. And then it suddenly hit her—in a flash she understood Søren's last clue. "Of course!" she cried. "That's what it means." She swerved the Mazda across two lanes and headed for the Western Avenue exit.

Impatiently Margit slowed down at the bottom of the off-ramp, anxious to turn around and find out whether her theory was right. She glanced briefly in her rearview mirror, and that's when she realized she was in trouble.

The silver diagonal on the front grillwork of the dark-colored car pulling up behind her was the unmistakable trademark of a Volvo.

Margit changed her mind about turning left and raced straight down the street. She zoomed through a yellow light, drove two more blocks, and took a sharp right at the corner. The Volvo was only a few yards behind her.

She stomped hard on the gas pedal, angrily goading the Mazda up the steep hill. She picked up the car phone to call the police but couldn't get a dial tone, and tossed the useless receiver onto the passenger seat. The rain was coming down harder, and the windshield wipers were swishing back and forth with the regularity of a metronome. Margit hunched forward to peer into the wet night, gripping the steering wheel tensely.

Clapton was just launching into "Breaking Point" on the tape deck as Margit headed for the Denny Triangle, a mangled crosshatch of one-way streets that was locally reputed to be as hazardous to cars as the Bermuda Triangle was to airplanes. It was her best bet for losing the Volvo.

Margit roared through all the red lights, took the turns too fast, and leaned on her horn as she swerved around vehicles blocking her way. She was hell on wheels, and for once she would have welcomed being stopped for reckless driving, but there wasn't a cop in sight.

She finally escaped the labyrinth of the Denny Triangle and headed down a deserted street near the AAA building. She glanced in her mirror. The Volvo was gone—it looked as if her plan had worked and she'd actually lost him. Margit tucked a stray lock of hair behind her ear and laughed with relief.

Then the Mazda decided to stall.

"Goddamn it," she cursed, shifting into neutral and frantically turning the key in the ignition. "Don't do this to me." She gave the engine more gas, but the only response was a nerve-wracking grinding sound.

"Come on," she insisted. "Start. You've got to start." She banged on the dashboard with her right hand, and then glanced in her rearview mirror again. There was the Volvo, just nosing its way around the corner two blocks behind her. He hadn't spotted her yet.

Margit desperately floored the gas pedal, but it was no use. She pulled out the key and decided to abandon ship. She grabbed her bag, jumped out of the car, and slammed the door shut.

Then she tore down the street, whipped left at the corner, and raced through the parking lot of some nameless manufacturing plant. She ran up the next street, not daring to look back, focusing all her attention on speed and forward momentum. She turned another corner, her lungs burning, and plowed right into the midst of a bunch of kids lined up in the rain outside Klub 9.

"Hey man, look where you're going," mumbled a guy wearing a soaked flannel shirt and baggy pants—Margit had rammed him hard in the back. His words were slurred and his eyes bleary, but he was trying to sound indignant.

"I'll give you twenty bucks for your ticket," gasped Margit, rummaging in her bag for her wallet.

"Huh?" said the kid, looking perplexed.

"Here," said Margit, waving a twenty in his face. "I need your ticket."

The kid gawked for a moment, and Margit thought she'd have to look for someone more coherent, when he suddenly grabbed the twenty and stuffed his ticket into her hand. Then he stumbled out of line and shuffled off. For eight bucks he could get himself another ticket and still see the show. And he'd have twelve dollars left to play with. That lady was crazy.

But Margit gratefully slipped into the safety of the crowd, huddling in the dark behind a young couple reeking of liquor. The woman was wearing a green vinyl raincoat and her date had on a black leather jacket with dozens of big metal zippers.

The line moved forward quickly, passing between two husky guys in red sweatshirts, who were efficiently frisking the crowd.

"Hey," said the woman in front of Margit. "Where's the female employee? Who's going to search *me*?"

The burly guy smiled and told her calmly, "We only do a waist patdown." He touched the woman's pockets, asked her what she had in them, and then swiftly ran his hands around her waist, from back to front. He did the same to Margit, and in spite of her panic, she couldn't help being amused that he felt the need to search a forty-year-old woman whose conventional appearance made her look like a librarian in the midst of all the extreme hairstyles and pierced skin.

Margit looked anxiously over her shoulder, but couldn't see the familiar thin form of Carsten Næslund anywhere. Maybe I actually ditched him, she thought with relief. But she was taking no chances, so she stepped inside the club.

Thick clouds of smoke circled overhead, filling the entire

room and choking Margit's lungs. For a moment she couldn't even believe she was still in Seattle—the scene was so astounding. She stood next to the wall in the back of the dimly-lit club and took it all in. There were shaved heads, tattooed heads, and hair dyed green or pitch-black. The women had glaring white faces and black-rimmed eyes, bright red lips and rings in their noses or eyebrows. The men were wearing leather jackets with silver studs around the armholes and spikes down the sleeves. They had on black leather gloves and heavy black boots. It was like the bar scene in *Star Wars*, filled with strange and horrific creatures, but Margit felt perfectly safe. She was invisible in this crowd—they simply didn't see her. She was too old and too straight.

Margit groaned softly and leaned limply against the wall, worn out and worried. She wondered whether Carsten had seen her come inside. She wondered how long she would have to stay.

Suddenly the band appeared on the small stage in front. The lead singer was as skinny as Mick Jagger, but Margit had no idea who he was. He was dressed entirely in black patent leather. He lay down on his back with the mike on top of him and screamed out the words of the song, but they were inaudibly buried in the crash of the music. The woman guitar player wore a leopard-skin tunic and leggings. She had enormous orange hair, and her earrings were dangling glass baubles that flashed red in the lights. Her face was emotionless, but her left thigh throbbed to the beat. The bass player seemed in a trance; the stark blonde hair, sharp profile, and flat chest gave no clue to the musician's gender. At the back of the stage the drummer slammed his sticks onto the drums, sweat flying, his hair plastered to his face.

Margit was momentarily mesmerized, but some quick movement in the shadows off to her left caught her eye, and she turned her head. There was Carsten Næslund, resolutely making his way through the crowd from the other side of the room. He was coming straight toward her.

Without even thinking, Margit rushed forward, shoving her way through the audience, and jumped up on stage. She pushed aside the bass player and nimbly evaded the grasp of a club employee intent on removing her. She dashed past the astonished roadies and groupies lounging in the wings, raced through the dingy Green Room, and practically fell through the door with the flickering red Exit sign.

A cab was just coming up the street, and Margit ran out to the curb to flag it down.

Before the vehicle even rolled to a stop, she wrenched open the back door, climbed into the seat, and shouted, "Pier 62. Hurry!"

The driver turned around to stare at the frantic passenger, his eyebrows raised so high that they almost touched the maroon fabric of the turban wound around his head. He had a bristly black beard, and the ends of his mustache were waxed into tight spirals.

"Get moving," she demanded, pounding her fist on the back of the seat. "What are you waiting for? Get out of here. Just go."

The cab driver gave her another brief glance in his rearview mirror, and then apparently decided that she wasn't a drunk or a deadbeat—just someone in a very big hurry. He pulled away from the curb with a squeal of tires.

Margit looked back and saw a dark figure emerge from the

exit of the club, but she couldn't tell whether it was Carsten or the frustrated bouncer.

Then she sank against the worn vinyl of the seat and closed her eyes, refusing to think about anything at all.

⌘

The cab stopped in front of Pier 62/63, and Margit got out on the street side. The rain had tapered off to a light drizzle, but there was still a brisk wind. She pulled up the collar of her jacket and bent down to hand the fare through the window, giving the driver a generous tip.

"Thank you, miss," said the driver, solemnly bobbing his turbanned head. Then he turned off the meter and moved the gearshift into drive.

"Hey, wait," said Margit before he could pull away. "Do you have a flashlight? Can I buy it from you?"

"I have one," said the driver, "but I need it."

"I'll give you a twenty for it. How about it?"

The man hesitated for a moment, as if calculating the replacement cost.

"Twenty-five," said Margit, glad that she'd stopped at the cash machine earlier in the day. This outing was really getting to be expensive.

"Twenty-five," agreed the taxi driver with a nod. He handed a cheap plastic flashlight out the window in exchange for Margit's money, and drove off.

Made himself a whopping profit on that deal, thought Margit as she stepped up onto the curb and stared after the disappearing cab. She stuffed the flashlight into her pocket, slung the strap of her shoulder bag diagonally across her chest, and pulled on her wool gloves.

Any other person would go home to dry clothes and a hot cup of tea, thought Margit. Any other person would head for the nearest pay phone to call the police.

But Margit was smoldering with rage, and that made her stubborn. In ten hellish days she'd been subjected to murder and mayhem—she'd been accused, threatened, and chased. Her normally quiet life as a freelance translator had been turned upside down and wrung out of shape. She'd been through too much to give up now, when she was so close to solving Søren's puzzle. First she would find the Golden Horn. Then she would march right into Detective Tristano's office and triumphantly place the ancient relic on his desk.

Margit turned toward the Sound, took a deep breath, and purposefully walked out onto the deserted pier.

17

Three tall streetlights along the sidewalk lit up the nearest strip of damp old boards coated with creosote. The rest of the vast expanse of the pier stretched into darkness.

Margit walked out to the middle and turned around to survey the site. She had a panoramic view of the city. In the distance the sleek glass buildings shimmered and the lights glittered with rain. She stared at the double-decker viaduct perched along the opposite slope and listened to the steady roar of the traffic. Her eyes moved to the Space Needle on her left and then back to the newly built condos in Belltown, their façades jagged with balconies. Off to the right she could make out the noble outline of the Smith Tower, once Seattle's landmark skyscraper, now overshadowed by buildings that looked three times its height.

So now what? thought Margit, dropping her gaze to the dark, empty pier. If she was right in thinking that the license plate numbers of the old VW pointed to this place, then where would Søren have hidden the horn?

There were four small wooden sheds set at intervals along the perimeter of the pier. Glass cases holding orange life preservers were fastened to their sides. A metal bar across the door of each shed was held in place with a padlock to keep out vandals. But Margit couldn't imagine Søren choosing such an obvious and easily breached hiding place. And she wondered whether the "XX" on the license plate meant anything.

What if Søren had arrived by water in his old skiff? Then he would have approached the end of the pier first, which was the least visible section from both the shore and the piers on either side. He probably came at night, but even at dusk or in the early morning hours he would have been reasonably protected from the view of any tourists at the aquarium or any workers at the construction site on the other side.

Margit turned around and walked out to the end of the pier. She leaned over the metal railing of the waist-high chainlink fence. The wind whipped her hair into her eyes, and she could hear the loud sloshing of the waves against the pilings underneath. It was a cold and miserable night, and she was beginning to wish that she'd gone on home instead. Just one more look around and then she'd call it quits.

Margit got out the flashlight and switched it on, running the beam along the outer edge of the fence. There were two metal ladders leading down into the water.

She walked over to the one on her right and instinctively glanced over her shoulder as she stuck the flashlight back in her pocket. There wasn't a soul in sight. Then she climbed over the fence and put her feet on the top rung of the ladder.

Halfway down, she pulled out the flashlight again and played the beam over the dank timbers and barnacle-encrusted posts under the pier. The spray of the waves soaked through the legs of her jeans and the back of her jacket. The damp wool of her gloves offered little protection to her numb fingers gripping the cold metal of the ladder.

Margit was about to give up when she suddenly caught sight of something white a few feet below her on a nearby piling. She aimed the flashlight on the spot, and in the instant when the waves receded, she saw the "XX."

With a gasp of excitement, she ran the beam of light up and down the huge rough post. On the back side, she could make out several handholds protruding from the wood like big steel staples—the kind sometimes seen on the side of water towers. She took another step down the ladder and leaned over, shining the flashlight along the underside of the pier.

And there it was. A large, black-painted box was lashed to the very top of the X-marked post, just underneath the planks.

"Yes!" cried Margit, making the beam of light dance in jubilant circles. But the thrill of discovery was quickly replaced by dismay. The post was barely ten feet to her right, but that wasn't close enough to reach from the ladder. She realized that the only way to get to it was through the water.

She told herself that the sensible thing to do was to wait until morning. She could go out to Fishermen's Terminal and ask Morris to bring her back here in his boat. Or better yet, she could tell Detective Tristano about her find, and he would call in a police vessel to recover the treasure.

Margit looked down at the restless waves and then shone the light up at the box again. It was too big a temptation—she couldn't wait. She was already soaking wet anyway. The water was choppy, but it was such a short distance, and in spite of her general lack of athletic prowess, she had always been a strong swimmer.

She stuffed her gloves in her pocket and then lifted her shoulder bag over her head and undid one end of the strap so she could tie it to the ladder. No sense in ruining all her ID with seawater. She debated whether to take off her shoes but decided she didn't want to risk cutting her feet on the barnacles or the rusty rungs on the post.

Then Margit took a firm grip on the flashlight, praying that it was waterproof, and lowered herself into the murky bay.

The water was so cold that it nearly robbed her of breath. Her teeth chattered violently, and for a moment she clung to the ladder with her left hand. Then she let go and pushed off to the right, making it across to the piling in a few swift strokes.

With a gasp Margit pulled herself out of the water and climbed the five rungs to the top of the post. She switched on the flashlight, relieved to find it still working, and examined the box. It would have been impossible to untie the damp knots of the thick rope holding it in place, but apparently Søren hadn't meant for the whole box to be removed. A hatch had been cut into the front, with hinges along the left side and a simple bolt on the right.

Margit shoved back the bolt, and then pulled open the hatch. The beam of her flashlight shone on a bulky oblong package inside, tightly wrapped in black plastic and tied with cord.

My God, thought Margit, there it is. The shock of actually finding something was almost more chilling than the cold of the waves. She had to put her hand out to touch the plastic before she could even believe it was real.

Carefully she pulled the package out of its hiding place and tucked it securely under her left arm. It was much heavier than she expected. She put the flashlight in her pocket, made her way back down the post, and clumsily plowed through the water to the metal ladder.

Shivering, Margit stepped up onto the lowest rung. She impatiently untied her shoulder bag and pitched it over the railing onto the pier above. Then she awkwardly climbed the rest of the way up the ladder, clutching the package to her side.

She hauled herself over the fence and dropped onto the pier. Her body felt like lead in the waterlogged clothes, and her feet squished unpleasantly in their sodden shoes. The wind stung her eyes, and for a moment her vision was fractured by the distant lights.

Out of the darkness a voice said softly, "Bravo."

Margit's eyes snapped into focus, and she found herself staring into the mocking face of Carsten Næslund. She felt so disoriented by his abrupt appearance that she thought she was looking at a disembodied spirit. Then she realized it was simply his dark clothing that made his figure seem to merge with the night.

"Thanks for doing all the work," said Carsten in Danish, his voice dripping with sarcasm. "Now hand it over." The sharp click of a switchblade warned Margit that he wasn't going to stand for any fooling around.

She hugged the wet package to her chest, her heart pounding erratically, her eyes blinking.

Margit couldn't believe this was happening to her—not after all the trouble that she'd gone to, not after she'd finally found what everyone else was looking for. It wasn't fair. Here she was, standing on a deserted pier on a dismal rainy night, soaking wet and cold, and all her efforts had been for naught. It just wasn't right. Sudden tears mixed with the rain and salt water on her cheeks, and against her will she opened her mouth and wailed her disappointment.

"Stop that," said Carsten with a menacing scowl. He took a step closer. "Cut that out. Nobody's going to hear you anyway. Face it—you've finally run out of luck. So give me the goddamn horn." And then he laughed cruelly.

It was the laugh that did it.

Blistering fury erupted through Margit's despair, and she did the only thing she could think of. She spat in his face.

Carsten flinched, swore fiercely, and then lunged forward, slashing the knuckles of Margit's right hand.

But he didn't notice her bag, which was still lying on the pier. He stumbled over it, slipped on the wet planks, and then fell. His momentary confusion gave Margit all the advantage she needed.

Holding tightly to the plastic-wrapped package, she threw herself over the railing and plunged back into the bay.

The cold dark water closed over her head, sucking her downward, and for a split second Margit almost succumbed to the pull of the depths. But she came to her senses and fought her way back to the surface, gasping and sputtering. The rough waves tossed her around, and she had a hard time staying afloat, weighted down as she was by both her clothing and the heavy package.

Then she heard a splash off to her right, and she realized that Carsten was in pursuit.

"No!" shrieked Margit, and she turned around, frantically starting to swim. But it was no use. With only one hand free, she could make little progress, and Carsten was gaining on her fast.

Margit felt him grab her left ankle, and then a fiery blade punctured her calf. He still had the knife. She gave him a vicious kick and managed to slip out of his grasp.

She pulled ahead a few yards, but it was obvious that she couldn't outswim him. In sheer desperation, Margit twisted around to face her pursuer, shifting her grip on the oblong package so that she was clutching one end with both hands.

When Carsten came within striking distance, she lifted the package high overhead, swiftly took her bearings, and brought it down hard.

It was too clumsy a weapon to aim effectively, and the surging water obstructed her view. But the edge of the heavy package glanced off Carsten's left temple, and the shock of the blow was apparently enough to stun him.

Margit saw him go under, bob up once, and then go under again. She didn't stick around to see any more. She thrashed through the waves to the other ladder on the end of the pier. In a daze, she clambered up the slippery rungs, still gripping the package in her left hand. Then she fell over the railing onto the rain-soaked planks and curled up on her side, unable to go any farther.

Margit had no idea how long she lay there. It could have been seconds, it could have been ten minutes or more. But suddenly she was surrounded by noise: a roaring car engine, pounding feet, shouting voices, splintering glass. And then the sickening wail of a police siren. A sharp light seemed to pierce through her brain, and she finally had to open her eyes.

The headlights of a car parked a few yards away flooded the area around her. She raised her head and squinted into the surrounding darkness. Shadowy figures were running along the edge of the pier, and then one of them jumped over the railing and vanished from sight.

The noise and commotion were too much for Margit. She groaned softly and buried her face in her arm.

Then someone was kneeling down next to her, saying something close to her ear. She heard her own name spoken over and over again, but the rest of the words were an incomprehensible buzz. She tried to reply, but all language escaped her; she was capable only of a strangled moan.

Someone tugged at her left arm. Someone tried to wrest the package out of her grasp. She protested feebly, but her strength was gone, and in the end she had to surrender.

Then someone lifted her up. She was swaying, rocking, hovering in midair. Nausea welled up inside her. She was seasick and dizzy. She refused to open her eyes. The chattering of her teeth rattled her jaw. She couldn't feel her hands or her feet.

Then the night caved in on her, and for the third time she sank into the depths.

Epilogue

F ive days later, Margit Andersson was sitting in the business-class section of an SAS plane about to depart for Copenhagen. She put on the headset of her Walkman, leaned back in the blue plush seat, and cautiously stretched out her legs in front of her. Then she raised the white plastic shade covering the small window on her left and glanced outside, noticing the hustle and bustle on the tarmac below.

She turned her head to the right and put out her bandaged hand to pat the big cardboard box strapped into the seat beside her with a special seatbelt extension, normally reserved for "EVPs" (extra volume passengers, as Margit's airline friend had once explained). But this particular passenger was a VIP, about to take off on the last leg of an extraordinary journey which had begun centuries ago when a remarkable goldsmith placed his exquisite handiwork in a Danish bog. Little did he know that images of his art would one day circulate around the globe, or that his name would be on the lips of millions of people.

Margit shook her head at the cunning hand of fate, which had lifted a reverent sacrifice out of the mud to test the limits of human greed. Three times the world had been offered a gift. Three times the world had failed to receive it. Now, incredibly, a fourth chance had been granted, and Margit found herself the unlikely messenger.

She laughed at her own sense of melodrama, gave the box another affectionate pat, and then turned up the volume of her tape. She was listening to the Eagles. She hummed along softly to "One of These Nights" and closed her eyes, thinking about the events of the past few days.

⌘

The first thing Margit saw when her mind swam back from the dim edges of consciousness was Renny's anxious face bending over her.

"Welcome back, kiddo," whispered Renny, putting out her hand to touch Margit's cheek gently. "How do you feel? You really gave us a scare."

"What happened? Where am I?" asked Margit, her mouth dry and cottony. It was a struggle to shape the words.

"You're in Harborview Hospital," Renny told her, propping a couple of pillows behind Margit's back so she could sit up. "Here, drink this." And she handed her friend a glass of water.

"You've been out for hours," continued Renny. "The medics brought you in around eleven, and the docs stitched up the knife wounds in your hand and leg. Don't worry—it's nothing serious, but you probably won't be able to type for a while. This sure hasn't been your week, has it?" She patted Margit's shoulder sympathetically as she set the water glass down on the table.

Margit gave Renny a woeful look. Her head was aching with the effort of trying to piece together everything that had happened. Images from the desolate pier were starting to come back to her. She raised her bandaged right hand to her face, wincing with pain as she smoothed back her hair.

"At first the docs were worried about hypothermia," Renny told her, "but apparently that wasn't a problem. They decided you were suffering from exposure and fatigue, but otherwise you're OK. They just wanted to keep you here overnight for observation. I think they might let you go home this afternoon."

"What time *is* it?" asked Margit, feeling thoroughly confused.

"Eight in the morning. The police called Liisa last night, and she came right over and then called me."

"Liisa is here?"

"She was, but she left around 3:30. Said she'd better get a few hours sleep because she had a big breakfast meeting scheduled with some Swedish software company. But you should have seen her with those docs. She is one fierce lady—insisted they explain all the tests and procedures. And she even got you a private room."

Margit was both touched and impressed by her boss's concern. She just hoped that her medical insurance would cover the extra expense.

Sunlight seeped in through the blinds and fell across the bed in thin stripes. Margit stared down at her lap, picking at a fold in the sheet with her left hand. Without looking up, she asked softly, "Did I kill him?"

"Good God, no," said Renny firmly. "Of course not. The cops fished Carsten out of the bay and, except for a big lump on his forehead, he's perfectly fine. He said you whacked him with that package you found. I guess he's been spilling his guts out to the police. Turned out to be a sniveling little coward as soon as they took his knife away from him. He told the cops that he found your business card in Søren's house—that's how he tracked you down. You know, I wish you had hit him a lot harder—a cracked skull and a mean concussion would have been fair trade for the stab wounds and everything else you've been through. Not to mention poor old Søren."

Margit leaned back weakly against the pillows, too relieved to reply. In spite of her vindictive fury over Søren's death, she didn't really believe in the philosophy of an eye for an eye. She didn't want anyone's blood on her hands. Not even a murderer's. Not even in self-defense.

"I want to go home," she said abruptly. "Can you get me out of here?"

"You bet," said Renny. She didn't care much for hospitals herself. "Just sit tight and I'll go find the nurse. Gregor is probably wondering what happened to you."

Margit spent the rest of Wednesday at home in bed, with Gregor curled up beside her. Renny popped in twice to see how she was doing, and Liisa called in the afternoon to wish her a speedy recovery. For once, she didn't say a word about work.

Around five o'clock, Lars and Derek came by with fresh-baked bread and a pot of homemade soup. As he dished up the soup, Lars told Margit that for the first time in history, Liisa had actually turned down a job.

"The police called the agency this morning," he said. "They needed an interpreter for their interrogation of Carsten Næslund. I guess he speaks good English, but the police didn't want to take any chances. If he claimed that he didn't understand something, it could jeopardize the whole case. Liisa told them she didn't have anyone available and referred them to Worldwide Language Services. I heard her say that myself. Imagine Liisa giving up a job to a competitor." Lars shook his head in amazement.

At seven that evening, Margit got a call from the police.

The officer told her that he was calling on behalf of Detective Tristano, who wanted to know whether she was feeling well enough to come down to headquarters the following morning. They were planning to open the package she had discovered, and the detective thought she might want to be present. Margit was surprised that they hadn't opened it yet, but apparently they were waiting for the Danish consul to get back in town from a business trip.

"Of course I'll be there," Margit assured the officer. "I wouldn't miss it." And besides, she had a few questions for the detective herself.

At ten o'clock on Thursday morning, a small crowd gathered in a cramped conference room in the Seattle police department building. Everyone was standing—they were all too restless with anticipation to sit down. Margit had brought Renny along with her, and Barbro had been invited too. There were a couple of men in three-piece suits who looked suspiciously like lawyers, as well as several police officers. Margit also recognized the Danish consul standing near the door. The room was overheated and stuffy, but no one even thought of complaining. All eyes were focused on the oblong package wrapped in black plastic lying in the center of the conference table.

Detective Tristano came into the room and brusquely said, "Good morning."

Margit noticed that he purposely avoided her eyes, and he seemed unusually nervous. I wonder what that's all about? she thought to herself.

Then the detective turned to the business at hand. He put on a pair of gloves, and with a sharp knife he cut off the securely knotted cords of the package. Carefully he sliced through the plastic and pulled it back, revealing several thick layers of styrofoam. He stripped away this second wrapping too, and underneath there was a dark red cloth bundled around a slender object.

The detective paused. No one in the room dared to breathe.

Then he folded back the cloth and everyone gasped. They were looking at the elegantly curved shape of the fourth Golden Horn.

Everybody started talking at once, everybody leaned closer to get a good look. Barbro pointed excitedly to the runes etched around the rim of the horn. "There it is, Margit! There's the inscription that Søren sent to you: 'I, runemaker, offer this horn.'"

Margit nodded and then pulled out a chair and sat down. She was suddenly feeling pale and weak.

Detective Tristano was at her side at once, saying her name and offering her a glass of water with unexpected solicitude. At that moment it dawned on her that he was the one who had knelt beside her on the pier, he was the one who had murmured her name over and over, he was the one who had lifted her up. But before she could ask him about it, the detective was gone.

It turned out that the police had been tailing Carsten, but they decided not to intervene until they saw both Margit and Carsten go over the side of the pier. Then Detective Tristano was called in, and he ordered immediate action.

"That guy's really loony about you," said Barbro a little while later as she and Margit and Renny walked out the front entrance of the building and into the bright sunshine.

"What guy?" asked Margit.

"The detective," said Barbro with a grin. "You mean you haven't noticed? I saw it the minute he showed up at the museum."

"You've got to be joking," protested Margit. "He's always sneering at me and giving me long lectures about my civic responsibilities. And besides, he can't be more than thirty."

"Guess he goes for older women," teased Barbro, giving her a wink. But Margit just shook her head in disbelief.

On Friday morning, Barbro and several other experts were allowed to examine the horn. Although they qualified their initial report by saying that they needed more time for study, they all cautiously agreed that the relic seemed authentic. And the runic inscription matched the style of runes on the horn discovered in 1734. The story made the front page of all the major newspapers, and the image of the ancient Golden Horn flashed over the news wires around the world.

Barbro told Margit that the discovery was doubly exciting because the dancing woman with the swirling hair in Søren's drawing was only one of several female figures engraved in the gold. This was a big surprise to the experts because, according to the drawings of the first two horns, only male figures had been represented. Was this due to censorship on the part of the early historians who made the first sketches? Or had the goldsmith suddenly decided to include women in his work? This discrepancy was going to keep scholars busy speculating for years.

On Friday afternoon, Margit received a call from the Danish ambassador in D.C., formally thanking her for recovering a national treasure. And then he invited her, at the embassy's expense, to return the Golden Horn to the Danish monarchy in person. Margit accepted at once, a little awed by the thought of an audience with the Queen.

⌘

Margit smiled at the idea of herself curtseying before the Royal Family. She certainly hoped that someone would fill her in on the necessary protocol in advance so she wouldn't seem too uncouth or boorish.

Then she took off the headset of her Walkman, slipped it into the seat pocket in front of her, and closed her eyes again. She settled herself more comfortably in the wide business-class seat. The plane had taken off and they were now steadily climbing toward cruising altitude.

Margit had managed to get hold of Joe on the phone the day before and tell him the whole incredible story. He had been astonished, incensed, fascinated, and appalled. He said he would come with her to Copenhagen, but she knew that he was in the middle of a new piece and really shouldn't leave. So she suppressed her own yearning for his company and declined his offer. It was comfort enough just hearing his voice.

And now here she was, on her way to Denmark with her famous traveling companion safely strapped into the seat beside her. The knife wound in her left leg ached and the fingers of her right hand were swollen and stiff, but otherwise Margit felt strangely invigorated.

She had successfully deciphered all of Søren's clues and tenaciously tracked down the ancient relic, which he had ended up entrusting to her care. Now she was about to right the wrong he had mentioned in his letter to the lawyer. The Golden Horn would be returned to its proper place, and the guilt that had turned Søren into a reclusive, secretive, and lonely old man would finally be absolved.

Margit had learned from Danish newspaper reports that Carsten's father had been one of Søren's comrades in the Tønder garrison when the Germans invaded Denmark in 1940. Søren apparently knew about his career with the National Museum, and decades later he tried to contact the senior Mr. Næslund about returning the horn. But by then it was too late—he was already dead. So Søren made the fatal mistake of confiding his mission to the son, unaware of Carsten's ambitious and unscrupulous character.

No one would ever find out how Søren came by the Golden Horn in the first place. No one would ever know whether he had found it himself in the fields around Gallehus where the other horns were discovered, or whether someone had given it to him for safekeeping and then was unable to take it back.

Carsten had already confessed to the murder, but he refused to give more than a sketchy account to the police. They still didn't know exactly what happened on that early Sunday morning when the old fisherman refused to give up his dangerous secret, and then paid for his recalcitrance with his life.

Margit sighed and opened her eyes.

A man wearing a dark blue blazer and gray slacks was sitting across the aisle, reading a newspaper. Margit blinked twice, thinking she must be seeing things. It was Detective Tristano.

"What are *you* doing here?" she asked in surprise.

"Official escort," said the detective gruffly. "At the request of the Danish government."

"And I suppose nobody else on the whole Seattle police force wanted a free trip to Copenhagen?" she asked wryly.

For the second time, Margit noted with satisfaction that she had actually made the detective blush. Maybe there's more to this guy after all, she thought. Underneath that unflappable professional façade.

"Just doing my job, Ms. Andersson," the detective said calmly, as he turned back to his newspaper. "Just doing my job."

Margit pulled out her Walkman from the seat pocket in front of her and put the headset back on. The Eagles were just starting in on "Lyin' Eyes."

It's going to be a long trip, thought Margit. But she wasn't entirely displeased.

Acknowledgments

Special thanks to the Seattle Public Library for allowing me to use the C. K. Poe Fratt Writers' Room, where *Runemaker* was conceived.

My thanks also to the authors and editors of the following reference works, which proved invaluable in writing this novel.

Guldhornene: En oversigt by Johannes Brøndsted (Copenhagen: Nationalmuseet, 1954).

A History of the Kingdom of Denmark by Palle Lauring, translated from the Danish by David Hohnen (Copenhagen: Høst & Søn, 1963).

Oldtidens ansigt edited by Poul Kjærum & Rikke Agnete Olsen, photographs by Lennart Larsen. Published in honor of the 50th birthday of Her Majesty, Queen Margrete II on April 16, 1990 (Det kongelige Nordiske Oldskriftselskab & Jysk Arkæologisk Selskab, 1990).

The Scandinavian Languages: An Introduction to Their History by Einar Haugen (Cambridge, Mass.: Harvard University Press, 1976).

Danmarks historie, volumes 1 & 14 (Copenhagen: Politikens Forlag, 1977).

A Book of Danish Verse translated from the Danish by S. Foster Damon & Robert Silliman Hilyer (New York: American-Scandinavian Foundation, 1922).

Tiina Nunnally has translated numerous prize-winning books from the Scandinavian languages, including three suspense novels. She lives in Seattle with her husband and cat. In her spare time she reads mysteries and listens to rock 'n' roll.

Other selected books from Fjord Press

Niels Lyhne
by Jens Peter Jacobsen
Translated from the Danish by Tiina Nunnally
$14.00 paperback

Mogens and Other Stories
by Jens Peter Jacobsen
Translated from the Danish by Tiina Nunnally
$12.00 paperback, $24.00 cloth

War
by Klaus Rifbjerg
Translated from the Danish by Steven T. Murray & Tiina Nunnally
$10.00 paperback, $20.00 cloth

Maija
by Tiina Nunnally
$12.00 paperback

Night Roamers and Other Stories
by Knut Hamsun
Translated from the Norwegian by Tiina Nunnally
$14.00 paperback, $21.95 cloth

Stolen Spring
by Hans Scherfig
Translated from the Danish by Frank Hugus
$7.95 paperback, $15.95 cloth

Please write, fax, or email for a free catalog:
Fjord Press, PO Box 16349, Seattle, WA 98116
fax (206) 938-1991 / email fjord@halcyon.com